Love Triology, Who To Complain

Devi Raghuvanshi

PARTRIDGE

To order additional copies of this book, contact
Partridge India
000 800 10062 62
orders.india@partridgepublishing.com

www.partridgepublishing.com/india

Contents

Dedication

Dedicated to my Parents, who made me to read and write, while they were just the farmers. Love you and miss you both.

Acknowledgements

I acknowledge and express my gratitude to my wife SUSHMA, for the input, spell check and all the inspiration and ideas, I conceived watching the degree of her patience.

My elder daughter PREETI deserves special mention for the emotional and financial support in bringing out the publication of both my books.

I would like PAYAL, my younger daughter to be a partner in my this endeavour. Frankly speaking I have copied some of her blogs to make my book rich and true.

Finally I thank all my friend on Facebook, my college mates, for encouraging me to write this book. My heartfelt thanks will not be complete unless I mentioned the big help I got from "Bhagvad Gita' and 'Google', the boss for anything.

You all are part of my these efforts and I have sincerely tried to bring the best in me.

Declaration

The contents of this book are wild imaginations of the author. Any resemblance of names, places or incidences are purely coincidental and unintentional.

The author does not take any responsibility for the loss or damage to anyone on account of publication of this book except he expresses his regrets for the damage if any.

DEVI RAGHUVANSHI

Chapter 1

Ajit was half sleep, half woken, eyes partially open. His pillow was soaked and it gave him a feeling of a wet pillow. Yes it was and it was due to continuous flow of saliva from his mouth. May be this must be happening once the moment he slept last night. Isn't that a habit normally kids have? May be he has a kid within him even at the age of 20. Nobody is surprised at home as they all know that he does it every day.

He was discussing with himself in sleep that saliva is an important part of a healthy body and it contains important substance that your body needs to digest the food and keeps your teeth strong. Human saliva is 99.5% water and other 0.5% consists of electrolytes, mucus, enzymes and anti-bacterial substance. Excess saliva may be due to overactive saliva glands or you have problem of swallowing, while this research was on and he was slowly coming out of his slumber, It suddenly gave him a jerk that something unusual is happening around him.

It could be around 8.00 in the morning, he could hear some loud shouts, commotions in the street below his house. For a moment he thought, it may be some procession like visarjan or early marriage celebrations in south Indian families. Since he was half woken up, it took him some time to understand and that it wasn't a procession or a marriage Celebration, it was an act of cruelty by some anti-social element like eve leasing of a girl or being victimized for being a girl. It was a case of sexual harassment or molestation.

He could not resist going down to find out inspite of repeated advice from all at home. His short temperament and hot blood drove him exactly near that inhuman act of Rehman, a local goon, history, sheeter and Shruti a teenage girl of his neighborhood. He was not known to either of them but decided to help the girl without knowing, who is wrong and who is right. He only thought that this could be done later but immediately, the girl is to be rescued. There were approximately 40 people both men and women but they were mere spectators.

A heavily inebriated man was hurling abuses. He pulled out this woman from an auto Rickshaw. She was on her way to the college. Rehman publicly assaulted her and abused her. He was so drunk that he couldn't stand straight. He was yelling with lewd comments like calling her a slut and all. The woman Shruti, upon enquiring about the incident said that 'she was on her way to college and this man shouted out item. I just asked him why he called me that?

Rehman was a repeat offender, a rapist and a threat to the society.

When asked the man why is he doing all this to this woman this was his response. What is your fucking business to interfere between us? Is she your sister, wife, mother or girl friend? He very politely told him, she is some body's daughter, she is a sister to somebody, she may be some body's girl friend or would be wife but on top of all this, she is a woman and needs his help in distress and that is all he is here for. Are you not aware who I am and which gang and influence I belong to? Are you not scared of anything or anybody? Are you not scared of your life or you do not have any body to cry for?

Now that is not your bloody business to know and I am not scared of anything or anybody so long as my inner conscience tells me that I am right and also understand that I am certainly not like any one of these standing here and tolerating your nonsense. This is the last time I am asking you to leave this girl and apologise and confirm that you will never behave this way with her otherwise I know what is to be done. As expected, he showed me the knife and threatened me to cut into pieces and parcel is to my mother. He again started yelling those filthy abuses which actually broke all barriers of my patience and I gave him few blows and he started bleeding from his mouth and nose.

While all this was happening the crowd did not react more than a show watch.

It was pathetic and pitiable to see the state of Shruti as the goon also called another accomplice who was holding Shruti and this guy was trying to stab me. I once again told him that I can give it a communal colour but I know that you are only a criminal not belonging to any community, caste or religion.

Some how Ajit pushed the girl towards the restaurant, a little away from the trouble site and he was immediately attacked by Rehman. He fought hard in spite of stab wound below his stomach. Perhaps he didn't realise that the cut is deep. The girl started screaming for help after seeing him seriously injured. The crowd increased but nobody dared to either save him or fight with the goons. The stab wounds were so severe that they were required to clip my intestines from falling and also there was one more grievous injury near his pelvic area. Luckily the brother of Shruti was returning from his classes so he took Shruti with him without making much noise and the police also reached the spot as may be, someone from the crowd must have called. Meanwhile Rehman and his accomplice had already run away from the site.

He was shifted to Nanavati Hospital by his family member along with the Police Van and Ambulance.

After completing the basis formalities of police and hospitals, he was taken to the operation theatre for emergency operation. It took 8 hours to complete the operation and was shifted to ICU for observations. The Doctors advised his parents that there could be some serious repercussions due to injury in his pelvic area which is connected to his urinary track or glands and reproduction system responsible for sexual needs. This all depends how his system reacts to the treatment. Ajit was advised post-operative care immediately after surgery for the duration of his stay in hospital and after his discharge from the hospital.

The biggest problem Ajit faced was increasing pain, swelling, repeated increase in abdomen pain, nausea or vomiting, fever and chilling sense and slight bleeding from rectum and wounds. After all operation of on the intestines colon and rectum are considered to be major surgery. It took him another two days to get out of pain and nauseating feeling. Even the blood thought rectum and wounds stopped and the family members were allowed to see him. By now Ajit was in a position to eat light and talk to the family and friends. Shruti visited him on fourth day. It was pitiable and she could hardly speak to him. All she said was, that she is responsible for Ajit's this condition and this guilt will stay with her life time. She said, Ajit, like other people you could also have stayed away from this, why did you do this to me? Had there been any other woman I would have done the same thing. 'Shruti, I am a mad man for right things. My parents and family are always unhappy with me for such incidences. Ajit looked on her mother's face who was also present with Ajit & Shruti. His mother told Shruti that he has never fought for himself or for reasons related with him and has always fought for others for valid and justified reasons. He lost his elder sister a couple of years back in such molestation and eve teasing cases at Marriot Hotel Juhu and ever after that, he has become like that. He loses his brains and doesn't tolerate anything against any woman.

Chapter 2

He was discharged after 15 days and was advised for no overdo and complete bed rest. For some weeks a care giver was also assigned to him for the dressing of his wounds and movement etc. After two weeks Ajit started returning to his normal life style. He missed his classes of engineering in IIT Mumbai for almost a month but was able to appear for his 6th Semester Examination. Ajit basically was a brilliant student so he passed his 3rd year B. Tech securing good marks and was promoted to the final year of engineering. The only thing, Ajit missed, during this period, was his inter collegiate badminton tournament which according to him, was a sure chance of winning the trophy.

Shruti was in constant touch with him during all these days and was happy for each and every movements of Ajit. It was because of this incident that Shruti became the part of his family and a very favourite person of Ajit's parents. They both, in there distant dreams, were also thinking that Shruti might become there future daughter in law, well, she would also be a qualified Chartered Accountant, good looking, a family type girl and on top of this she is also from the same city. So dreaming this, was not something out of box. Ajits mother, sometimes used to hint Shruti the possibility of this alliance. It was Shruti who told his parents to check with Ajit as Ajit normally talks about Sudha, his classmate, very enthusstically. Sudha is very beautiful with brains and beauty. She has waist length hair and a pretty face, Shruti used to joke around and tell Ajit that girls don't get selected for IIT for their looks so obviously Sudha must be rare for both beauty and brains and Ajit used to pass it as a casual observation but at the same time he never proved also that it is a casual remark. He never even expressed it. Ajit's mother said, normally he discusses everything at home. He has not done it even once. I will check with him to night.

Chapter 3

Ajit infront of Mother (ANJALI)

Ajit finished his dinner with his parents, the mom prepared rice chicken roti, Raita and Kheer specially for him as he used to always say that I don't need any sweets after meals if I get kheer made by my mother. As the mom wanted her son to reveal some secrets so everything was done as per his taste and likes. His father left for evening stroll with his friends so this was the right occasion to rope him in her net as he will not speak an iota of words when his father being there and that too specially about his classmate so called his girlfriend. Who is this girl Sudha, Ajju? asked the mom. Ajit was taken for a big surprise and shock. Who Sudha Maa? He tried his best to dodge the question but Maa was firm and asked Ajit, come to the point straight away and let me know everything about Sudha. Who told you about Sudha? That is not important who told me that. I would like to hear it from horse's mouth. Maa, may be that mad girl Sudha, she must have only unfolded that mystery of the universe. I very casually discussed with her my classmates including Sudha. Why she only told you about Sudha and why not about Aakash, Sunil, Atharva etc.? Ajju, don't beat around the bush. Let me know the facts and figures about Sudha only. I don't mind meeting her it I find things in order.

It is nothing like that Mom and you need not meet her or any other girl. If need be I will inform you well in advance and you can pick and choose your daughter in law to be. I seem to be confused Ajju but let me know whatever little I must know now. Shruti will never speak a word other than asked for or other than required. You have so much faith in that mad girl. Maa, I agree she is a sweet girl, matured enough to tell the truth. I have a special liking for Sudha for her nature and guts to face the reality of life.

Ajju, you are again taking me round and round by discussing Shruti which is not required now so before your dad comes and you become dumb, tell me about Sudha, Ok. Mom, are you ready with your sharp mind and investigative eyes? Yes, go on. Well, Mom, Sudha is a Rajput girl from Delhi. Her father is commander in Indian Navy so she has come from a decent family with open mind. She is an intelligent girl who has won May ball Navy twice. Navy ball is like miss India contest for unmarried girls of Navy families. We have been together from 1st year onward in same branch of computer engineering. We are assisting each other for sessionals and practicals. During my this crisis of hospitalization, she has helped me for covering up all academic activities like journals and practicals. There is nothing more than this, Maa.

I would like to share with you that there are many classmates and college mates, seniors and juniors who want to be friendly with Sudha but she finds me more sober and civilized. Yes, by your this discussion, my attentions now is drawn and driven to her to ascertain whether she can become my girlfriend or your future daughter in – law. Shruti is aware of all this but probably she and you both have over estimated our alliance. Let Shruti come, I will take her class for diverting my attention. Chill Ajju, you don't have to ask her anything. She is a very simple and pure soul. In any case she is coming tomorrow evening to help me for my interior decoration work at home.

Ok Maa, I have told you and raised the curtain from my love story so called and now keep this secret in your heart and do not discuss with big boss, Thakur Saab [Vikram S. Tomar] my dad, otherwise he will also be ready with his guns and roses. Ok. I will not talk to him but if I come to know anything more than that what you have told me I will hand you over to him for his ways of guns & noses. Ok. Good night Maa.

Chapter 4

Next Day in College

Everyone says that engineers are logical people and say that everything has a formula and a solution but can they deal with love can they use there mathematical ways for understanding love? Simply big NO and for Ajit, it is 100 percent NO. Ajit entered the class and was behaving like a thief caught by the cops with no eye contact with his classmates including Sudha. He wanted to sit on other side of the Class which was far away from the seat where Sudha was sitting. Sudha felt a bit awkward. She just winked and signalled him to come and sit close to her. Are you having conjunctivitis or what? You are not at all looking at me why? He didn't have answer. Like a stupid, He said just like that. Has Shruti asked you not to look at me or what? There is something definitely, Ajit, you are hiding. She was constantly teasing and provoking him and the poor chap was sitting quiet like a NINCOMPOOP.

Anyway professor Vishawanathan started his lecture on logics for software development. Professor Vishawanthan was bearing a maroon coat and a very loose trousers which I think, his father must have left after his death. Always a serious type, miles away from Smile, even his wife must have not seen him smiling anytime. By the face value he was bad photo copy of Sir EINSTEIN.

Sudha was waiting for the classes to get over before she could take on this character called Ajit.

With great difficulty Ajit gathered courage and told Sudha everything that happened yesterday evening. While Sudha was anxiously composed and listening, Ajit was telling her like a confessional statement in a church. No doubts, she was shocked but she also boldly told Ajit that when I sometimes look at you, I feel that you are not too bad. You can pass my examination with few grace marks. Ajit thought in his mind, that he would score 100 out of 100.

Both of them were normal in and out of the college, but a seed was born in their hearts and they both knowingly or unknowingly started thinking about each other. For both of them, it appeared to be a case of love at first sight.. Was it love or infatuation like your other half pulls you towards her like the opposite poles of a magnet or was it a sympathy towards him? he knew and Sudha also knew that love is the foundation of families and stable societies where lust is a physical emotion that we act upon in the heat of the moment.

Does she care for him not just in words but in action? Does she have time for him, thinks about your plan and goals in life? Do I or does she know that this is healthy relationship including open to change to the process of facing and accepting uncomfortable emotions and situation? Only time will tell. They became more communicative to each other not only in matters related to their studies but also about there professional career and family affairs. At times they used to score one up on each other and Ajit used to get a bit uneasy and used to ask Sudha, when I talk about sine wave, you go on tangent and when I talk of love, you start talking about your sister losing a smart phone. What is all this Sudha? Same with you also Ajit when I talk of hardware you talk of software. Ok, Sudha let us not discuss hardware and software as it is too technical but yes do you know the similarity or difference between a woman and a computer? Ajit asked. Sudha only said shut up. We are still students beginners as boyfriend and girlfriend. We are certainly not husband and wife ok? Yes I know.

It has been six months that Ajit and Sudha have been together in the changed relationship and a lot has changed over the last six months between them. Ajit has been like a lost kid and Sudha still the intriguing and beautiful girl he met almost years back. Yes today they are together and rest of the world, does not matter to them what they do and what they think about them. They are sitting in an open Café of the college and exploring their past and future. Sudha in her torn black jeans and while top and Ajit as usual in his white shirt and grey trousers which was his national dress. They were sitting under some big banyan tree. Her hair blew in all directions in the evening breeze; Ajit for the first time caught Sudha's hand and he felt that somewhere reaching out and taking Sudha's hand is beginning of a journey, felt as millions of tiny universes being born and could feel the adrenal rush in him and probably in her also.

Chapter 5

Two Weeks Later

Ajit and Sudha were looking forward for one month's educational cum pleasure trip to North India. Normally engineering students of 3rd & 4th year go out on such trips every year. It is always a pleasure to travel with your beloved and have some time for your own, away from your busy life of engineering college days. Leisure, pleasure and educational trips are best ways to take yourself to nice places with options like scenic beauty beaches, hill stations. North India offers something for everyone including NOIDA and Gurgaon for training in computer science and also places like Manali, Dharamshala, Dalhousie, Shimla offer a great deal of relief from scorching heat and sweat of Mumbai. They both were very excited and happy that they would be together day and night for a month. This feeling of being together rather made both of them a bit more romantic. Sudha cautioned Ajit to behave and not become wild during this tour. Ajit assured her that he will take good care of his doll and protect her from all internal, external evils including cold of the weather also. Sudha asked him how would you protect me from cold? This is confidential and I will tell you only when we both face it. Shut up, was the reply of Sudha. As scheduled, a Central Railway bogie with 75 berths was booked and this became the temporary home for the class mates for a month. The train started on 16th Jan at 4 pm from Mumbai, VT. Now called Chhatrapati Shivaji Terminus. Ajit was on lower berth and Sudha also on lower berth opposite Ajit. The journey started...

The journey was rich specially for Ajit and Sudha. Everybody was moving in the coach from one birth to another except these two guys with an endless conversation on everything except engineering. It started raining after Nasik. The view was wonderful. The Western Ghats are rich and if it rains, the journey becomes more magical. The greenery looks refreshed with so many streams and waterfalls. The best stretch is between Nasik and Itarsi as the train passes through paddy fields and tunnels. They reached Bhopal early morning. Sudha asked Ajit "do you have anything else to do except following me even in my sleep with your roving eyes. I could not help it Sudha as you have actually now become a habit of my life, Ajit said. I knew you will say the same thing you are a windbag. Ok. What would you like to have for breakfast asked Ajit. Sudha Said, one cup of Coffee, Egg Bhurji and two toasts. Look ahead Ajit on this platform there seems to be a nice snacks joint.

Ajit brought two plates of breakfast and Coffee and said, anything for you Sudha. Sudha said I do not really know whether the stuff was tasty or it has become tastier after seeing you running on platform to fetch it. Actually you, Ajit and a big thank you.

Next stoppage was at AGRA. Whatever type of tour you plan, there is entertainment and also an element of education. Place to visit Agra was not to be missed. Ajit told Sudha that you cannot think of Agra without thinking of Taj Mahal as it is a monument of love. Taj was constructed by Shah Jahan in memory of his beloved wife Mumtaz Mahal. By now Sudha started understanding why Ajit is insisting on words like monument of love, beloved wife and her senses started working for Ajit's advancing togetherness. Ajit continued, the Taj stands for brilliant architecture of Moughal era and named as one of the wonders of world and heritage.

Agra Fort is another site you will never like to miss. It is close to Taj Mahal and is situated near the garden of Taj Mahal. It is also known as Red Fort of Agra. This fort comprises of many palaces of moughal architecture. Shah Jahan used to spend his last days here viewing Taj Monument from here when he was kept as a prisoner by his son Aurangzeb.

Sudha was in agreement and disagreement also as he liked basic idea of construction of

Taj Mahal for his wife as true symbol of love but expressed agony and unhappiness on Aurangzeb for arresting his own father. Bloody cruel. In a lighter mood, she asked Ajit what you would have done in case you would have been Shah Jahan, for your wife? A long breath, silence, Ajit said that in case Sudha would have been Mumtaz, I would have opened minimum a Taj Cyber Café and small Taj Restaurant. That is nice of a thought for you but I will not compromise for anything less than a Taj Mahal.

They took a bus to visit Fatehpur Sikri which was built by Akbar as a tribute to a Sufi Saint. It is a mix of Indian Islamic and Persian architecture and made of sand stone. Itmad-Ud-Daulah is one more addition to moughal architecture. Now Sudha, do not ask me to make Fetehpur Sikri just to get a son. Don't day dream, proceed, we have to reach to our home, sweet home that is railway bogie before 9 pm. It was a bit tiring but a satisfied day for both of them. They were happy and seemed partially committed to each other.

Next stoppage was DELHI.

Since Sudha was from Delhi and she knew the place very well, she told Ajit at Delhi railway station only that Ajit, this is my empire and everything will happen as per my whims and fantasies. You have to just hold my finger like a kid and I will take you around Delhi. She told Ajit that we will go to Chitranjan Park, meet my parents have breakfast take Papa's car and roam around Delhi, come back home in the evening, stay with my parents and next day morning, reach Railway station at 8.00 am before the train leaves for Chandigarh. Ajit was confused for staying overnight at Sudha place, but was given no option so he said ok. Sudha asked Ajit what do I introduce you as to my mummy Papa and why you only at home why not remaining 69 students?

You can tell than that this is Ajit, your future Son-in-law and presently a trainee boyfriend to their marvelous, beautiful daughter. O, Hello Ajit, stop day dreaming. What if they take it seriously in word and spirit? No, they will not as they know that only a blind man, with no brains will many you and will go for self-destruction. Shut up and in the same conversation mood, they reached at Sudha's place at Chitranjan Park.

As expected, mom and dad were waiting outside and both greeted Sudha and Ajit with a solid hug. Ajit never expected that commander Singh is such a simple jovial person that he did not feel awkward ever for a second and concluded that Sudha carries both her mom and dad in her and she is a wonderful woman because of them. Sudha winked at Ajit and told mummy daddy that he is Ajit, my classmate, my partner in all my projects and he is quite a help in our studies and extra-curricular activities. What is your full name, Sudha's father asked?

Ajit Singh Tomar, originally from Gwalior and parents, now settled in Mumbai. That Singh and Tomar gave him an extra confidence for some parental thoughts.

Both Ajit and Sudha had breakfast, a typical Delhi style, nice Aloo ke Parathe, white butter, curd and mango pickle. Both of them enjoyed it to the fullest and left for Delhi Darshan in while Hyundai Verna Car. Sudha was on wheels as she was conversant with Delhi type driving.

They first visited Qutub Minar which was close to her house. What a piece of architecture? Ajit quipped. Sudha told him that it was built by Qutub-UD-Din Aibak in 12th Centure with red stone as a sign of Muslim domination in Delhi. It is 72.5 metre high and you can see the staircase nicely carved. Ajit do you know or remember that famous song "Dil ka Bhanwar Kare Pukar, Pyar ka Raag Suno, filmed on Devanand and Nutan in film Tere Ghar Ke Saamne. This was done on these stairs only. Ajit started singing and acting like Devanand and Sudha followed the rest of the act. Ajit was quite happy and excited. His scale of love towards Sudha rose one notch. Since they did not have much time. So they avoided deep studies on carvings and verses of Quran.

On their way, they saw India gate and Rajpath famous for Republic Day Parade. They also saw Sansad Bhavan, Rastrapati Bhavan, Connaught Place. Sudha also showed him the area where terrorists attacked parliament. It was 2 O'clock in the afternoon so Sudha look Ajit to Bhape Di Hattee, a very famous non vegetarian food joint of Connaught Place. They both ate nice Chicken Tandoori which Ajit never tasted in Mumbai to match the taste. They took a casual round of Janpath and Palika Bazar and did some shopping. Ajit gifted a beautiful pen to Sudha with "WE TWO" written on it.

Now they headed for NOIDA, INTEL knowledge Centre and spent close to two hours understanding CHIP designing and assembly of hardware for computers, TVS and BMW cars. Sudha saw the chip making for the first time so compared chip with Lijjat Papad. They both returned to Chitranjan Park at 8 pm, quite tired and exhausted. Sudha told him that there are many tourist places in Delhi but we could choose the few important ones.

After a hot bath they all assembled in the drawing room before dinner. Sudha's father CDR Ajay Singh Chauhan, introduced himself to Ajit as an original native of Jaipur and 'Now settled more or less in Delhi. His elder son Abhay is in U.S. working for Tata Consultancy Service TCS as the branch head in LA and he is to retire from Indian Navy in two years from now. My wife Vinita is vice principal in Central School in Hauz Khas Delhi. Ajit also introduced himself that I have my father a retired I.P.S. officer and mother a housewife. I had an elder sister who was molested by some goon in Mumbai and she committed suicide. We are now settled in Mumbai and we have considerable agricultural land in Gwalior. Ajit felt at home after meeting Mr. & Mrs. Chauhan.

They both were dropped at the railway station by Cdr Chauhan.

The journey again started.

It look after 5 hours for our train to reach Chandigarh. Ajit was showing the nice and colourful crops of wheat and Sarson and entire journey was giving them a pleasant look of yellow flowers and Sudha was appreciating the nature's beauty from the moving train. This time it was Sudha, who was explaining Chandigarh to Ajit. She told Ajit that Chandigarh is the best planned city of India for its architecture and quality of life. It's capital for both Punjab and Haryana states. It is an epitome of modern civilization and serenity created as green revolution. With its proximity to Mohali Punjab and Punchkula Haryana makes it Chandigarh TRICITY. The city was planned by American planner albert Mayor and Swiss French architect LECORBUSIER. Beautiful Roads educational institutions are the highlights of the city. Lakes and artificial gardens are added attractions. The only bad news is for smokers that either they do not find a Cigarette shop anywhere or may be in some hidden corner of a busy market.

I hope, Ajit you don't smoke and like the city. Yes I just loved this city and I feel we can settle in this city said Ajit. We? You can think of settling in this city not me as there are hardly any career possibilities in Chandigarh. No I.T. projects, hardly any industries. But yes, if you want to open a garment shop or a restaurant, after your B. Tech, degree from IIT, you can settle down here.

They roamed around all the sectors, lakes. Did boat riding in the lake and enjoyed few moments of their togetherness in private. Ajit held her hand and said very confidently for the first time that Sudha you are really very beautiful and amazingly intelligent woman. So what? I just wanted to convey feeling and thoughts whatever came to my mind through heart. I never knew that you could be that romantic some time but remember, we are students only. Ok. Now no more lectures please Ajit told her angrily. From Chandigarh they look a route to Kalka and Shimla. The journey between Kalka and Shimla was very beautiful for scenic beauty but scary too as it offers steepest rise of altitude. It passes through more than 100 tunnels and 800 bridges with picturesque Shivalik Mountains and green trees like OAK, pine and maple. This really made their journey memorable. They could feel the freshness in air. Sudha was a bit scared of the Tunnels and bridges especially due to darkness in tunnels. She actually hugged and held Ajit tightly out of fear and Ajit thanked the situation and prayed that this journey never ends. Sudha only understood it after reaching Shimla that Ajit has actually encashed the opportunities of the situation and ambience but she didn't feel bad.

Chapter 6

In Shimla

Ajit was sitting on a wooden bench in one corner after reaching Shimla. Everyone was enjoying walk on the mall Road which was the only place in Shimla where tourists and locals are normally seen in the evenings. Seeing him alone, quiet and lost, Sudha asked him what is bothering him? He simply brushed aside the question and told Sudha that he is feeling home sick. Sudha knew that this is not the case and there must be something in his mind which may be, he doesn't want to share. Sudha by nature is kind and concerned person so she insisted on knowing from Ajit. He also could avoid anybody except Sudha so he hesitantly had to open up.

Sudha, it is good to love and there is nothing beautiful than a fulfilling relationship and many things of my last relationships solidified my positive view on love and relationship. I must confess that I am not totally mad at you. I am just sad that you are locked up in that little world of yours. And when I try knocking on the door, you just sort of look up for a second and go right back inside. I love that feeling of being in love. The effect of having butterflies when you wake up in the morning that's special. I am in love with you and you can't blame gravity for falling in love. Sudha, feeling the low nerves in Ajit. Put her hand on his shoulder. Please do not put your hand on my shoulder as your touch is so divine and sends waves down the back of my neck. What exactly do you want was the next question of Sudha. I want to be a couple as he and you are no more teenager to joke around. His voice was firm and defiant. Ajit stared deep into her eyes and said, I have to avoid looking at your face and eyes as much as possible because when I do it, all I want to do, is to kiss you. Sudha again repeated, I need time I will like to see the future of our relationship. Can we take to next level? Everything between them started off casual. Sudha confessed that she too has some feelings for Ajit but I have certain reservations being a girl and a daughter. Ajit said that you are my love and to be honest that feeling will never fade. As long as you are in my life my heart, my mind my soul my spirit, you will remain. Sudha interrupted and asked to clarify his as long as ……….. how long? Hope it doesn't become null and void the moment we reach back Mumbai after this trip? Till destiny or death aparts us, was the answer. Satisfied and overjoyed, they both went for very satisfying meals in the nearby restaurant.

While having meals Sudha said that Ajit, I am a matured girl and I also do not want to hurt you but fact remains that I have a very strong liking for you, I am also emotionally attached with you but committing for a permanent alliance will not be proper at this stage for two reasons. One we are still students and young in age, two I still need time to make me understand you and your people. I agreed that love has no age, no limit and no death. Ajit asked Sudha that tell me with conviction on whether you love me? Reply came AD-RIB from Sudha, Why are you becoming wild and restless? Is today the last day and world will be doomed and there will be nobody on earth including you and me? No doubts, I don't say that I love you but you know it pretty well that you have become the habit of my life. They proceeded to Srinagar from there. They visited Srinagar, the moughal gardens, Gulmarg, Pahalgaon. The places are so beautiful with gardens, very friendly people, vast lakes and pristine streams and stunning landscapes that they both agreed that if there is heaven or earth, it is here only. They both had a Shikara ride in DAL lake and they for the first time felt that they are a couple. Ajit became over protective to Sudha. While travelling in a cab from Srinagar to Pahalgaon, Ajit asked the car's driver why there is too much of unrest in Kashmir and you see deployment of Indian Army all over? The car's driver was also the owner of that Taxi service. He said that they have lost a lot of business due to this unrest or terrorism.

Ajit did not hesitate is asking what exactly you all want or what are your demands? The driver was quick to respond to say "Azadi". We want independence from India. Ajit asked him that if it is not possible which is almost a certainty, would you like to stay with India or Pakistan? India of course. Pakistan is a failed state. They also saw the place from where Amarnath Yatra starts.

They returned to Mumbai, by Amritsar Mumbai Express. Sudha went to her hostel and Ajit back come. Yes, the feeling of separation was felt by both though it was temporary.

Chapter 7

Shruti When Ajit Was on Tour

Shruti was busy in her own studies but became silent and was not speaking much unless provoked to speak. She used to visit Ajit's mom and used to enquire about Ajit and family's wellbeing. There was not even a day when she did not make tea and help cooking his mother. In fact she had made a place in his mom's heart. Once when Ajit's mom was having high fever, suspected viral or typhoid, she did not leave her even for a second. She stayed with her after taking leave from her college and office. Ajit's mother was so much emotionally charged that she said. I have lost my daughter couple of years back but I have got her back in you, Shruti.

She thought to herself that Shruti is the perfect definition of an ideal lady and true realization of womanhood. She has an average looks but very strong virtues – innocence, Sincerity and devotion. She is kind, helpful and shy too. The most interesting part about Shruti is that you may not like her in first glance but when you gradually know her, your likeness for her will turn into serious love. In my opinion Shruti is kind of girl rarely found. She wished if an alliance is made between Shruti and Ajit, she would consider her one of the luckiest mom. She may not be good as girlfriend of Ajit but will make a perfect wife. She said that Ajit, the stupid guy, understands this and comes to my terms of relationship. She even expressed her this desire to Shruti and Shruti very confidently answered, Aunty, don't worry. I am your daughter in any case if not a daughter-in-law.

Shruti in her wild imaginations asked herself that what does she look in her future husband. Well, tall, dark and handsome, has now been replaced by broadminded understanding and caring type. Compatibility should be an important factor. When I think of Ajit I do not find any of these thing missing. He could be a real partner for marriage. But whether he loves or he doesn't at least I love him or I have a passion for him. Let destiny decide and let me see what is slated for me in future. Let him come back. I will discuss with him and resolve disagreements if any. I don't know what I am doing here? Do I love him? I will learn to love him. I know that

"Love doesn't start in the morning,
and doesn't end in the evening,
it starts when you don't need it,
and ends when you need it the most."
I will, I will, I will.

Chapter 8

Ajit was at home for a week before his final exams and campus interviews were supposed to commence. Shruti came face to face with him for the first time, he came back from his educational trip.

Ajit -   How are you Shruti, long time we met, we didn't even talk? How are your classes and job going on?

He was looking constantly at Shruti. Shruti was in her best look with white Salwar kameez and colourful Lahariya Jaipur Dupatta. She was looking gorgeous without any make up. Actually Shruti had big black eyes, long hair and a very impressive personality.

I am doing good my studies and job are fine, I have my final exams for C.A. How was your trip? Hope you did not overdo it with your class mates specially Sudha and all? By the way how is she? Actually you wanted to know more about Sudha rather than me? She is fine and is in the hostel now. Mom was highly appreciative of you and was mentioning about what you did for her. I should thank you from my heart. You are such a wonderful human being. Even dad was mentioning that you were a great help for both of them. He normally doesn't appreciate anybody but he did it. What magic you have done on them? Do a bit of 'it on me, I will remain indebted to you throughout. Are you pulling my legs by being so sarcastic or is that your natural way of taking Panga with me? Asked Shruti. No I was just joking Shruti. I appreciate you as a complete woman and a friend. Shruti sensed an extra flow of blood in her nerves. She thought that Ajit is either a wordsmith or he has me in his thoughts some times.

Chapter 9

Campus Interview

Ajit and Sudha were sitting in Coffee Café day CCD in Powai near their college campus. Sudha said to Ajit. Ajit it has been lot of fun relaxation and too personal intimate discussion during our trip but don't you think, this is high time we get back to our work. We have campus pre placement interviews in just about two weeks from now. Everybody is working hard to get the best of placements. Ajit said yes, Sudha we also have to plan our placements. But you were talking about doing your masters either in U.S. or MBA in one of the IIM so what then?

I have two options one to appear for campus interview and try to be with you in one company or if it doesn't work, then go in for either MS or MBA. Why can't you make up your mind? You could still be with me even when you do MBA but yes if you go abroad for MS then I am not very sure whether you will even remember me. It is going to be minimum two years. In two years you will be seen with some white skinned blonde. You are like that only. No Sudha, you will always remain with me here or there and yes, there could be possibility that you and your that white skinned blonde, might share everything of mine including me. You are so generous, with big heart to accommodate her also. Is it ok for you? Shut up and stop day dreaming. Let's now concentrate first on campus interviews then on the final examinations. By the way, let me make it clear to you that I don't play second fiddle to anybody I will never be a second choice to you or to anybody. Ok, ok, enough, let me get you the list of companies and their programme tomorrow and sit together to find strategy to interview and till then no romance, no music, no language of love, no couple. Sudha smiled and said yes. We will.

Next day Ajit went to the college and gathered all the details of the companies and their itinerary and informed Sudha to make best resume for both of them. He informed her that following companies will be coming to campus for recruitments.

1. T C S
2. Infosys
3. Wipro
4. HCL
5. Mphasis
6. Patni computers
7. Cognizant
8. Accenture
9. J. P. Morgan
10. Reliance Industries
11. City Bank

12. Facebook

These companies will be conducting interview in next three weeks.

He also explained Sudha how these interview will be held. She was listening to Ajit like a good Student.

The following is going to be schedule of interviews in general but some companies might skip one or two steps.

1. Written Test - It will be for non-technical subjects, like aptitude test for maths puzzles. Some companies will conduct written test purely on technical subjects like DBMS, Software engg., JAVA, digital electronics and computer architecture.

2. Technical - will mostly be on the project Interview undertaken in final year.

3. GD/Essay - this group discussion will be writing conducted in batches of 8 to 10 students and its aim is to ascertain the leadership qualities.

4. H. R. round - We may be asked some routine questions like tell us something about yourself, where do you see yourself after 5 years from now. Before all said above, will generally be replacement talk where the companies will enlighten about their history, accomplishments, major services offered or products. They will also inform procedure, financial package and service bond if any.

They both got their resume made from a Professional Company.

Ajit also bought white shirts, grey trousers, black shoes and dark colour matching tie. He also bought blue coloured blazer and became a gentleman candidate.

Sudha purchased two sets of dress, Indian and Western outfits. Indian dress consisted of a light coloured Cotton Sarees, Salwar Kameez with plain Dupatta. In Western dress, she got plain light coloured blouse with formal trouser and one skirt of knee height and a matching blazer. She also gave an impression of a smart corporate staff.

As schedule Sudha appeared for Accenture and appeared in all tests including personal appearance to Accenture team. They were all impressed with her technical knowledge and smart presentation. She was offered package of Rs. 20 lacs per annum she informed Ajit about the interview and told him that he will be selected by all companies wherever he appears. They are my father-in-law or what? You seem to be so confident. She blushed with word father-in-law but said, ok, go as if you are meeting your father-in-law, done.

Ajit had Reliance first and he scored the highest marks in written test, GD and personal appearance. He was offered 12 lacs per annum. A surge of anger ran through his entire body and told the company bosses. Sir go down south of Maharashtra that Shinde's college of engineering. You might get your choice of engineers or go to some polytechnic college for diploma holders, your wish will be fulfilled. Please note that if you offer peanuts, you will get monkeys. He thanked them and left the interviews. This was not appreciated even by the college placement officer but what to do, Ajit is like that only.

Next day, was another interview for both Ajit & Sudha for Citibank. Sudha requested him not to lose his temper with these people. Ok, I will remain calm. You are a sweet darling said Sudha to him, just to keep him in good humour. Ajit cleared all tests and interviews and was placed second after Ashish, another class mate and Sudha was 4th. Ajit was offered 32 lacs and Sudha 25 lacs. They both discussed pros and cons of the offer including two years bond. They both decided to join Citibank at Mumbai after final examination.

They both celebrated their achievement and went to Lonavla to celebrate. They univocally said that any crusade requires optimism and ambition to aim high. Ajit became emotional and asked Sudha, will you always remember me and be my 4 am buddy? Yes I will, under any circumstances good, bad, worse or joyous and they for the first time united in body and soul. No regrets from either end for breaking their resolution of no romance, no cupid or whatsoever. Sudha began to tie her disheveled tresses into a knot and asked Ajit, to leave for Mumbai after breakfast.

Ajit knew that Sudha has a child in her and she understands me better and I expect her togetherness at all times. There is a soul between us who is as dear as she is and cannot be neglected without a guilt. Guilt for what? It is an unavoidable love with no feeling of return. She loves me or not who cares? At least I love her and will continue doing so till destiny creates a wall but then who cares. Ajit only asked Sudha, do we carry a guilt? Not exactly because whatever has happened, has happened in the spur of a moment and it was a consensual sex. So let it be but I will talk to my parents after the exams.

Chapter 10

Preparations for final exams

Ajit and Sudha did not find it difficult as they were concentrating from the start of final semester. They also found it easy and stress free an they prepared on the basis of previous years exam papers, specially for last five years. All new chapters they learnt from YouTube videos as it is easy to understand from video formats. Another advantage they noticed by this study from YouTube, was that if had up dated information on subjects rather than conventional books.

One of their professors also suggested them a noble way of teaching each other. they both divided the entire syllabus in two parts that decided that Ajit will master 1st half and teach Sudha and Sudha the second part and teach Ajit. Though this system puts an extra pressure on both of them but it was a positive pressure. They followed this system and if came out to be handy, Ajit asked questions which Sudha answered and vice verse. By teaching each other revisions were done number of times. They also learnt about sweet sections of the syllabus.

Sweet section is the portion of syllabus that carry more marks. They made a list of this sweet section based on question asked in last five years. After studying this, they both concluded that sweet sections question are mostly derived from standard question and answers.

Sudha advised Ajit to concentrate on hand writing as he had a habit of doctor's hand writing.

In between preparations, they used to go to late night tea joints. By having tea, they thought that they can remain alert to study more. Ajit's mind then was concentrating on Sudha's beauty and cupid was working all the time with him. once they were caught at late night near tea joint by patrolling cops but Ajit managed to please the cops by referring his father's position as an ex IPS officer and also by passing some Indian currency to them. Sudha asked Ajit, can we study now seriously as your job is done. you feel happy and alert now? He kept quiet for some time and actually lost in the books. Ajit was partly serious in studies but Sudha ensured that this idiot studies.

They studied for two months together every day. They both did well in the exams. When the result came, they both stood first and second in IIT and in fact she stood first and Ajit second. They both wanted to celebrate together. They had gone to MINI Punjab in Hiranandani and ordered some Fish Tikka and Paneer Chilly as starter. On Ajit's insistence Sudha also accepted to taste vodka with orange Juice and finally ordered two Tandoori Paratha and desi murg curry as main course. The food was good and so was the ambience for both of them to sit in a cozy corner all by themselves. Ajit was in no mood of feeling anything but love. Ajit said to Sudha that you are my love and to be honest that feeling will never fade. I know Sudha replied. I understand your feelings I respect them. How about celebrating our success with our parents? My parents are coming to Mumbai after two weeks for a family function so we can meet both the parties and some communication link could be established between both the families. What do you say? The idea is excellent Ajit said. Sudha aksed him whether your parents will not behave like parents of Krish Malhotra of two states? No dear they, are as simple as me. So I have to be more careful because you are a dangerous man in gentle crowd. I have seen you twice as wild as it could be. No, not the least, I am wild only in romance with you otherwise I am a cow type soul. This arrangement was fixed for next week in club called G.C.C. at Mira Road through a very close friend and class mate Aakash.

During the entire discussion, Ajit was constantly looking into Sudha's eyes which were his weakness as they were magical in his words. Nor did his this romance fulfill his deepest desires. Not content with mere friendship Ajit was searching for the ideal union of body and soul that has escaped him in his adulthood. He embraced this quest with passion and urgency. They both kissed each other, hugged lightly and separated to their respective destination homes.

Chapter 11

Sudha joined Citibank

After one week Sudha joined Citibank at Mumbai and made arrangements to stay at YMCA girl hostel. Ajit requested her to stay at her place but she too politely refused the invitation. They both knew the reason of Sudha not staying at Ajits place. Ajit was in two minds whether to join Citibank or wait till his CAT exam results for admission to IIMS are out. Ajit told his parents, Sudha and Shruti that if he once joins Citibank, he has to undergo a service bond of minimum two years and he will not be able to complete his MBA. He was also due to appear for IAS exams in next four weeks.

Finally decided not to join Citibank and wait for what was stored in his future. Sudha was disappointed and irritated at his decision. But Ajit was firm and explained to Sudha that he would like to pursue further Studies or go in for IAS jobs. Though Sudha was not convinced but agreed with him and wished him all luck. Shruti whole heartedly supported Ajit for his doing MBA specially in any IIM. She saw a much better future after his MBA even in companies like Citibank or Facebook etc. Shruti was genuine in thinking on these line and also partly due to selfish motive of Ajit staying away from Sudha. She never realized that their relationship might take a much deeper root because of distance but Shruti was serious but confident.

Chapter 12

After two weeks

Sudha's parents landed in Mumbai early morning. Both Ajit and Sudha had gone to receive them at domestic airport. Chauhans were looking happy to see Ajit more than they saw Sudha. Both of them hugged Ajit which gave Sudha reassuring feeling for Ajit. Ajit said, Uncle Aunty why have you booked yourself in Hyatt Regency Hotel? Our house is big enough for you to stay. Ajay with a smile on his face said may be next time, we will stay with your parents. They all checked in Hyatt Regency and decided to meet in the evening at G. C. C. club Mira Road at 8 pm.

Vinita asked Ajay, What does he feel about Ajit? I know what you are intending to ask me but yes in case both Ajit & Sudha feel that they could be couple in future, the match would be good. Let us also meet Tomars in the evening and feel their state of mind. I only hope that they are as gentle as Ajit and should not behave like typical Gwalior Tomars like Man Singh Tomar. Ok. But do not boast too much about your achievements etc. no, I will be a nice guy after all he is going to be our son-in-law in case things work out. But did you clearly talk to Sudha about her acceptance of Ajit. Yes she says that Ajit could be a right man in her life. She has heard about his mother. She is a simple domestic type lady but his father is a typical Rana Pratap type but Ajit says that he can manage him. keeping their fingers crossed with hopes or no hopes Sudhas parents reached G.C.C. at 8 pm. Vinita was wearing a typical Rajasthani Saree Lahariya type and a rich Rajpootana make up and the Ajay is a black suite with white shirt and red tie. Sudha was in a colourful silk Salwar Kameez and a very beautiful contrast Dupatta. Ajit received them in reception lobby and informed them that Mummy Papa are expected within next 30 minutes. Meanwhile he took them around G.C.C. showed them blue sparkling clean swimming pool, health club, T.T. & badminton courts, Billiard, Tennis court and the guest rooms. They liked the entire set up of the club and an idea started working in their mind that marriage can take place in this club if granted by God. Ajay asked Sudha, how did you like this club? Excellent Papa, this is one of the best places for party function. Thus they indirectly obtained Sudha's approval. Ajit was too excited to take them on all the places explaining different activities of the Club. Sudha pulled him back without the knowledge of his parents and passed a lovely comments. Ajit so much of butter in not required for my people.

I have already done the homework for you. Really? Thank you and I am sure you are also going to do the same thing when my parents arrive.

Meanwhile they were informed by reception that Tomars have arrived and are waiting in the lobby for Chauhans, This club was not new as they have attended many marriage parties and cocktail dinners in the past.

Ajit finally introduced his parents with Sudha parents and a signal of mutual acceptance was felt by both Ajit and Sudha in the first glance.

Their meeting and dinner were arranged in private dining room which could accommodate app. 10 people. A beautifully decorated hall, beautiful furniture and soothing interiors, made the taste of the evening a notch higher. Both Ajay and Vikram started talking about their roots initial education and career etc. While they were discussing their school education, they found out that they both were from St. Laurence School Sanawar in Kasuali hills of Himachal Pradesh. This union of theirs brought them so close that they started talking like two lost friends. Ajay was two years Junior to Vikram. Their mothers also chatting about everything under the sun from their cooking to kids. Anjali also told Vinita about the tragic death of her elder daughter. They mixed up so well that they forgot the basic purpose of their meeting. Ajit told Sudha yaar, is it about us or the old people are having a ball time?

Ajit ordered some drinks and starters for all. The blue level Whisky was preferred by two men, breezer by Vinita and orange juice by Anjai. Ajit and Sudha ordered fresh lime water with soda, sweet and Sour, Ajit wanted to impress his would be in-laws but the plan was foiled by Sudha who orderd vodka with orange Juice for Ajit. Some nice Tandoori Fish Tikka, was hot and paneer Tikka was also served. They all appreciated Ajit's choice of starter. I only taught him to order all this things Papa. I knew this will be liked by both parent's, said Sudha. Very funny replied Ajit.

How is your Job going on Sudha? Asked Ajit's father. If appears nice uncle so far and it is only a week or so but Citi looks one of the best corporate in world. The office is good and comfortable attractive so I feel, I can think of a good career with them. That's nice and then looked at Ajit. You have left that option but we do not have complaints as you are now a matured guy. Ajay asked Ajit, what was the reason for your this action Ajit, if you want to share with me. Papa, before he tells you anything, I will tell you, Ajit is different, unique, will never follow crowd and will always do something HATKE. Ajit's father agreed and said, Sudha, you know this brat very well.

Well somebody give me space to say some things please? Anjali said, Go on Beta, let my little one explain. Everybody laughed on his being called little one including Ajit. Ok. When I was appearing for my campus interview. I was not very keen on a 10 to 5 desk Job, as a project or product manager either in a software company or as a banker. I was more inclined to do field jobs like fighting, sand mafia, stone mafia, oil mafia or land grabbers as I had heard too much about, IAS officers being killed or thrashed by all these anti-social elements. As such I decided to join IAS cadre. The second option, I had, was do some research in development of nuclear power or science like Dr. Kalam. I have already appeared for IAS exams and results are due any time next week and I am hopeful of my selection as conventionally first 50 ranks are always achieved by engineers scoring 100 out of 100 marks. You will do it Ajit, Ajay and Vikram univocally said which was seconded by all three ladies. Lastly if all I have to join Citibank like companies, I will join after my MBA.

Sudha said, it is better for you to join Citibank after MBA otherwise I can become your boss and give you lot of trouble. You are my boss even now as I hardly get an opportunity to say something when you speak said Ajit.

Everybody enjoyed the meals and meeting and before leaving the private dining room. Both the parents asked Ajit and Sudha, regarding their engagement in plain language whether they both agree to this alliance? Yes, we both respect your thought and thank you for being so kind and considerate. They left the club with a promise too meet again in Delhi for future programme as nothing could be done now till Ajit takes a final call.

See you tomorrow after your office said Ajit. Yeah! Day after tomorrow. I am spending a day with Mummy Papa tomorrow. You don't come to hotel as they talk to you more than me. Feeling jealous? Yes, specially mom, Arre, she is your fan. She says that he is very quiet unlike Sudha and good looking, well-mannered and all. She has forgotten other adjective otherwise you would have been loaded with them also. Why you don't feel the same about me? Asked Ajit. A sort of, yes, replied Sudha, you are ok. But not that much as they describe you. Movie day after. There is a nice movie in INOX INORBIT MALL very romantic, a bit adult. I know why you are inviting me for that movie. You will like two corner seats in the theater and apply all your antics on me but I will be with you there anyway. You are a cute mischievous guy and at times, I love your these mischiefs. Bye for now.

Next day Ajit only joined them at airport to wish them safe flight and bye uncle, aunty.

Chapter 13

After Three Days

After three days, he got his results for MBA. He scored good rank but not good enough to be in IIM Ahmedabad and IIM, Calcutta. He got his third preference at IIM Indore. He shared this information first with Sudha then to his parents and Sudha conveyed to her parents. He was to join at Indore within next 7 days. Sudha was happy for him. Ajit sent his acceptance to IIM Indore. Indore was a known place to them as Vikram was originally from Gwalior.

Ajit called up Sudha – Hi sweet heart Su, is short name for Sudha, used first-time by him. now since I am leaving after 7 days I feel we should spend some quality time together. I will miss you Ajit as now I have started feeling the pain of living without you for some time. Sudha's voice was choking. She said that there is no specific reason why first love is so powerful. It is always filled with intensity and passion and you start thinking that they will last forever. This makes sense because this is the first time you truly love and feel loved outside your family. I have never confessed to you Ajit but today I feel like telling you that your absence will make a lot of difference in my life.

Ajit sensing the serious mood of his girlfriend, wanted to change the mood and told Sudha that now since I will not be there with you for a period of considerable time and you will have lot of smart good looking guys in Citibank. If should not happen that one day, when I meet you, you say, who you? Or Ajit meet Vijay, my immediate boss and my new boyfriend.

Ajit, I am not in mood of listening to your such crap. I trust that a man is lucky if he is the first love of a woman and a woman is lucky if she is last love of man. For me loving you is like everything else in life, should be a discovery an adventure and like most adventures you don't know until you are right in middle of it. I will come with you for your shopping of new dresses and important things needed in hostel at Indore. I will miss you all the time Ajit and Ajit will miss Sudha all the time.

Ajit also met Shruti at his house and told her, Shruti, I need not tell you because it is in your DNA to take initiative and responsibility. Since, I am not with my parents all the time for next two years, I will depend on you to take care of my parents and keep me posted for everything. I know that you are more close to them specially my mom so I have no fears for anything but please keep on talking to dad as now he has mellowed down and needs some words of sympathy and company to talk. Ajit, go without any stress, I will try to ensure that they are looked after as much as you would have done.

Chapter 14

Ajit Left For Indore

Ajit reached IIM Indore and took a week to settle down in ambience of students and friends seven of them from Mumbai. College was good, hostel excellent and people in Indore, simple helpful and nonaggressive like Mumbaikars. City was peaceful. Nice places to eat if your hostel mess is closed specially Sarafa Bazar. Good sweets and chaat to eat in the late evenings.

Ajit explored two things in life being alone. One missing his family and Sudha and second exploring philosophy of life like your goal to be best in whatever you do and never be afraid of failure and ways to lead by his own examples. He set goals with deadlines for success in everything and respect time wisely. He always tried to lead by example. He never tried to motivate himself by talking as he believed that words ever meant as much as action. His schedule at IIM was worse than hectic for studies presentation. He used to say that every day he tells the birds to chirp or get up. He agreed that hard work never fails.

He also has to maintain his long distance relationship LDR with Sudha as he is aware that long distance relationship in an intimate relationship between two people who are staying in different cities. He devised ways to maintain this. Hi, Sudha how are you doing? Sudha replied Real Gold is not afraid of test of fire so our distance will not pull us apart but bring both of us together. But still Sudha, there are some ground rules to manage our expectations. I need you physically also that is why I am talking dirty with you. Do you understand that sexual desire is like a glue that keep both of us from drifting apart. Not only this is a biological need, it is an emotional one as well. Sudha jokingly told Ajit, do not throw me in web of your words and concentrate on your objective. You have life time to perform your beasty desires.

Ajit kept the flame burning by teasing texts filled with sexual INNOENDOS and provocative descriptions to Sudha. He used to tell Sudha that now only one and half year left to meet you as and when. They were in constant touch on Whats'app and viber and used to talk everything under the sun for hours together upto wee hours.

Sudha, I am coming for two days next Saturday and Sunday so no work, no excuse, we will be on our project only. Ok, I will wait for you Ajit, as after all the waiting and yearning and abstinence I will be meeting my prince charming. Now get back to your studies dude. Bye Sudha.

As scheduled Ajit came and met Sudha, lunch, movies, little things like kissing holding hands, being intimate were the highlights of two days. Both were honest to each other and shared the deepest secrets and desires.

Sudha while seeing him off at railway station, reassured Ajit and said, Ajit distance means so little when someone means so much. We are the perfect couple. We are just not in the perfect situation for now.

Ajit sentimentally told Sudha that when you feel alone, just look at the spaces between your fingers, remember that in these spaces, you can see my fingers locked with yours forever. Yes, the thought of being with you tomorrow gives me strength to go on today Sudha sealed her conversation turned back and left the train without seeing him again. Two drops of tears rolled down.

The same night, she sent him a message 'I see the stars' but without you, they look only stones scattered.

Chapter 15

Two Months Later

Ajit called up Anjali, Maa, I do not know today, I was remembering you both. May be the work pressure, I was home sick so decided to talk to maa, the only cure for my mental and physical fatigue.

How are you, mumma & papa? Is all well with your health? Does Shruti come and meet you?

We are perfectly fine beta. How are you and your studies? We know it is very stressful and tiring for you but we are so confident on you that you will make it.

In spite of her hectic schedule, Sudha never keeps me waiting. She is no longer glued to her laptop or cell phone. She is often there to help me with my cooking or laying table. She is there to solve our problems and plan the things for tomorrow. She takes interest right from medication, disciplining and cheering up your dad. She is by my side for anything, be it sickness. Last week she has taken both of us for a nice Hindi movie. She is turned VIVACIOUS and caring with lot of enthusiasm and energy. Yesterday her parents also came home on tea and we had a lovely evening.

Ajit, she is a wonderful girl, like part of our family.

Good, maa, I trust her so much.

Bye Maa,

Bye Ajit, Papa says bye beta.

Chapter 16

Trial of Rehman

During all these months, Rehman was jailed and tried for attempt to murder and out raging the modesty of a woman and also under many other sections of I.P.C. Ajit and Shruti were called only twice as the Honourable Court exempted them for the reasons of Ajit being away in Indore, exams and Shruti being alone.

In between Rehman expressed desire of meeting Ajit once before the judgment is announced which after getting acceptance from Ajit, was granted. Ajit was accompanied by Shruti to meet Rehman in the presence of honorable judge and police. Rehman said to Ajit. I do not know what will be the outcome of my court case but I had a desire to express my regret to you that you were no way responsible for the entire incident. You only helped madam and suffered a lot. You never had any personal interest but for the sake of an human act, you jumped in the browl. I seek an apology from you now so that at least I will not live with one guilt of harming you for no personal gains.

Ajit -   Do you really think so? Do you feel that you will never do it again? I have pardoned you. Let Shruti and court take the right course of action.

Shurkiya, Sir, Rehman told.

He was sent for two years rigorous imprisonment and honorable court took a lenient view on this case.

Chapter 17

Ajit in Final Year

The life in final year was still tough and required time management at all times including time for your bath and meals. Sometimes you have to miss either of two or both. Life at IIM Indore was hectic frenetic but it was never dull. Here everything, every activities are managed by students be it mess, committees, functions or social gatherings. Since all the students are based in the campus so there are classes till ungodly hours. Mid night, sessions and constant pressure to deliver. The campus never sleeps like Mumbai. If is also compulsory to participate in sports, birthday celebration to have strong friendship and a desire to be a leader.

As a routine classes start at 8.30 am so you have to face heavy crowd in the mess. Not only does one has to be on time but also to be prepared to have studies previous days lectures. The 15 minutes tea break after 75 minute lecture is the only solace. The professors are, Gods and are mostly from big corporates or from big Govt. sectors. Summarizing above the students have everything except time for themselves. Ajit managed all aspects of life and also achieved the distinction of being the best badminton player of all IIMS. All this happened because Ajit never became part of the problems and remained committed to creating new life for himself and also kept concentration on responsibility, honesty and integrity. For him his family, including Sudha, Shruti were the institution.

Inspite of Ajit having such monotonus life, he never forgot to speak to Sudha. One such conversation. Sudha, I have been in love with you for years. Since the first time I saw you in my 1st B Tech class in Mumbai, if was me who wanted to meet you but you wouldn't let me come close to you. Some times to that extent that I though I was never going to meet you. You are not mad asked Sudha or are you kidding. Sudha gave Ajit a strange look then. Never do that again. Ajit, now only few months left, please concentrate on studies. I am not running away.

No yaar, I was just kidding and making my mood better so that I could finish all my chapters for the second time. Love you, bye sweet heart. Bye Ajju.

Chapter 18

Campus Interview And Final Exam

In a face book interview at Indore, Ajit was told that they have a personal belief that whole world does not need to know your personal business. They just needed you and offered Ajit a position of Manager infrastructure in Mumbai and also offered a package of Rs. 75 lac per year subject to clearing his MBA and his acceptance of one year service bond. Hiring the right candidate for the right jobs is a technical process and requires significant skill on the part of HR team and they have done it in his case. Ajit in fact has been booked rather than selected leaving all the formal tests like written test, aptitude test, GD and personal interview. Ajit's record of all his last examination was a basis for their faith in him. He was advised to join on or before 15th July. Ajit thanked all the people including top brass of face book from U. S.

He had only four weeks for his final exam. He again sunk himself in the books and related google search which paid him the dividends. Ajit cleared his MBA and secured second rank. He shared his this achievement with his parents, Sudha and Shruti as well. Everyone was on cloud 9 hearing about his results. Ajit's father congratulated his son and said, Ajju, I knew it, you will do it though I never expressed, in public, Son, the proudest moment for me is telling the world that you are my son. I love you now and forever. Now forget about IAS and join the main stream of work now. We have certain responsibility for you to be discharged within next six months. I have already talked to Chauhans and Sudha also. I have seen the happiness, glow and pride on her face after your achievements. Now she says, yes Ajju has become a boss. Ajju now come quickly after completing all your pending issues there. I will be waiting to see you and your mom now wants to see you as early as yesterday.

Yes, Paa, I will be there in a weeks' time. Bye.

Chapter 19

First Day at Face Book Office

Ajit after joining face book was given briefing about the company. the Senior Vice President Charles from U. S. head office addressed him and another twenty managers. He started that Facebook's mission to make the world more open and connected is only one percent. We are looking for talented people who are hungry to build new things and bold enough to tackle complex issues that make the world better for everyone. We move fast at face book so you have opportunity to make an impact on your first day and every day after.

So best of luck. We will now break for lunch and after that you all are at your own. Ajit had the lunch with the entire team. The food and service was from Trident. So it has to be good and Ajit's career started from that day.

Ajit was given the responsibility of heading the real estate division of Face book. The primary aim was to acquire office premises on lease, outright purchase, carrying out interiors with furniture and fixtures on pan India basis. His this job profile involved lot of travelling all over India middle East and Singapore etc. It was a challenging assignment and Ajit was enjoying it thoroughly.

Chapter 20

First Meeting With Sudha After Joining Face Book

For Ajit love in most powerful, magical force in the 'universe and it displays its beauty and wonder more than in the intimate relationship between two people. No matter what is written about our relationship one thing is sure that when love enters our lives, it never leaves without transforming us at the very depth of our being. he hesitated for a moment but could not resist calling Sudha.

Ajit   - Hi, Su what's up?

Sudha - Just taken a shower and drying my tresses, than breakfast, tell me what are you doing?

Ajit   - With wet hair on your shoulder, you must be looking like a temptation for me to have a look at you.

Sudha - Come over we will have breakfast and lunch together.

Ajit   -   No, you come over to Inorbit Malad.
              We will have breakfast, inorbit lunch
              and movie today. I promise, no wild
              actions. I also have to tell you about
              my office.
Sudha -   Ok, I will be there in next 45
              minutes, Bye.
Ajit   -   Bye darling.

Ajit was standing on second floor near the
Escalator in the mall and when he saw Sudha
on the ground floor, taking the Escalator, he
was continuously chasing her steps. Sudha
was looking very cute with white top and grey
skirt, black shoes. Her hair were long and style
magically arranged. She was looking like a
college student in uniform. He waved her to
come fast and expected escalator to become a
high speed elevator. She look another escalator
from first floor to second floor and reached him.
The guy seemed overjoyed and excited. He,
without waiting, hugged Sudha tightly, making
her a bit embarrassed but he didn't care. Held
her hand till they reached food court specially
only Paratha's. Sudha said you may have been
a cop in your last birth as you are not leaving
my hand only a hand cuff is missing. I am not
running away dude. Sorry Sudha for a moment
I forgot that we are in a mall. They had stuffed
Parathas of Potatoes spinach with curd. Ajit had
already purchased movie tickets of DDLJ and
entered INOX in mall at 12 noon.

Ajit	-	Sudha, Facebook is nice office, I am responsible for its real estate division and have to travel a lot within India and outside. Staff over there is well educated and well behaved but yes some attitude, ego problem can be noticed as they are all professionally qualified and highly paid.
Sudha	-	How many girls are there associated with your division.
Ajit	-	Eight all from North India, smart and good looking and are single except one. Ajit told her.
Sudha	-	So hope, you will concentrate on your work rather than those smart, good looking girls.
Ajit	-	Nobody is as beautiful as you are and pressed her palm. You better be careful, you know that I am an independent and follow logics.
Ajit	-	Nothing could be done now as both the old couples have agreed to see us husband and wife.
Sudha	-	Ok how is the work pressure?

Ajit   - A bit tough but manageable, much less that what it used to be at IIM Indore. The movie was good but throughout the movie there was another set of SRK and Kajol behaving and doing exactly what the actual hero and heroine were doing.

After the movie, they left to their homes and before leaving, Sudha told Ajit let us not meet too frequently. My mom advised me this. It may not be good to meet more often before marriage. Ok. But today at least we must meet in body and soul. Said Ajit. Shut up and just go away before your web of words takes me in trap. Bye.

Bye Sudha, call you to night. I miss you.

I miss you too Ajit.

Chapter 21

Shruti & Her Status

Shruti by nature is calm and composed but exceptionally good looking by any standards. She will never open up unless provoked to speak but this doesn't mean she does not have feelings of love, affection and respect. She is a qualified Chartered Accountant leading a team of 30 staff in one of the best accounting company. She has started loving Ajit but keeping it to herself forcibly as she does not find it too easy and possible most of the times.

She thinks that love is more than just being married to or making love to someone. Millions of people get married millions of people have sex-but only few are real lovers. So to be a real lover, one must commit, be loyal and true to your partner. You are a true lover when you feel that whatever happens between both the partners is significant and everything you say in relationship has the potential to cause your beloved joy or sorrow and everything you do, will either strengthen or weaken your relationship.

Shruti believes that true love is an all-encompassing emotion and is beyond possession or ownership on Ajit. She was matured enough to understand his uniqueness and would mould her into forms suitable to circumstances. She was always there with Ajit's family. Ajit was also very close to her and very affectionate to Shruti. He used to miss her if she was not around. Same with Shruti but the relation was far different then the relationship between Sudha and Ajit. Ajit was not having an iota of knowledge that Shruti in her wildest dreams, might think about an adult relationship between them. Ajit accidently touched Shruti many times, But that adrenal rush of blood caused by cupid was not there till now.

Anjali in spite of so much discussion between them and also seeing the status of serious involvement between Ajit and Sudha was still in deep down the thoughts, considering Shruti as a probable daughter –in-law She knew it that it is now a distant dream yes. She agrees that if you close your eyes this doesn't mean that sun has set. Ankhaen Band Karne Se Suryast Nahi Hota.

Chapter 22

Discussion Between Tomars And Chauhans

After a week both vikram and Anjali took a morning flight to Delhi to meet Chauhans to discuss the programme and normal rituals being followed in Rajput marriages. Upon reaching Delhi airport they were received by Ajay Singh and were escorted to Sudha's place, at chitranjan Park. Vinita welcomed them with Aarti and applying Tilak. Normally this is done when the relationship is formally established but Sudha's mother did it with a confidence of this happening shortly. The parents from the Boy's side become VIP's.

Tomars were there with them for just one day so both the families discussed the programme in details. Accordingly to the programme the marriage will take place in NAVAL Auditorium and lawns in Delhi followed by reception there. All together there will be approximately 50 people travelling from Mumbai to Delhi to Mumbai by Rajdhani express and Ajay will arrange through his contacts in ministry of Railways. Both Ajay and Vikram being Friends there will be no dowry except all arrangements in Delhi will be done by Ajay and all arrangement in Mumbai by Vikram. All rituals old and new will be religiously followed by both sides. The marriage will take place exactly after 40 days from today.

As good gesture of celebration, both the Thakurs had drinks and dinner at Ajay's place and left for Mumbai the next day.

Chapter 23

Matching of Horoscopes of Both

As a first ritual, it was decided by both the families to match the horoscopes of both Sudha and Ajit. Ajay sent his daughter's horoscope to Vikram. An expert future teller was called and both Ajit and Sudha were asked not to be party for this enigmatic research and development.

Ajit - Sudha do you believe in all this?

Sudha - Not 100 percent but what is the harm in knowing it and satisfying our parents.

Ajit - What if they don't match?

Sudha - Jokingly, I will go as per fortune letter's advice.

Ajit - I do not trust all this, even if they do not match even one percent, I am not going to leave you.

Sudha - So am I also baby. Why do you become panicky so fast. Have trust on yourself and if not, at least trust me. I am a stronger woman.

Ajit - Sure na! ok. If that is the case, let us enjoy the entire exercise.

In the evening when they both reached home, Ajit's father was normal but mom was looking tired and worried.

What mom? Horoscopes didn't match or what? His father answered. Look it is very difficult to match horoscopes of two people. Our's also did not match but we are happily together since last 30 years.

So their fears came true. Both Ajit and Sudha spoke in one voice to see the mysterious documents.

Ajit's Horoscope	-	Your sun sign is water sign of Scorpio. This makes you intense and passionate. This also makes you a man of surrender, acceptance and inner focus on sacrifice and growth.
Sudha's Horoscope	-	She is born on the cusp of Libra and Scorpio. She will have the charm of a Libra and passion of Scorpio. She is attractive. She will always be pulled in two different directions of the head and the heart. She is romantic.

Summery   -   With Sudha, even though you have been living together, I do not see a great deal of harmony. You give in because you are not able to withstand her reactions and move. Even though you do not voice it, there is a deep resentment and disappointments. The marriage will withstand the test of time.

Ajit   -   There is nothing new in this, we are both aware of it. She is strong headed but is always correct and justified. She doesn't stand fake and untrue things. I am an Amoeba and would cover her and protect her from all evils and all poignant circumstances. Maa, Papa, do not worry for anything. We have accepted each other in all ambience like Gold shines only on the test of fire.

Both the parents were contented on their statements. In the same way Sudha convinced her parents and they knew no amplitude of joy.

Chapter 24

Tragedy Begins

One day when Ajit was returning from his office, after attending a daylong seminar, he felt some pain in his lower abdomen. By the time he reached home, it became acute. He thought, it may be due to appendicitis or may be stone in kidney. Within no time, it reached to that extent that he was admitted to Leelavati Hospital in Bandra.

He was put on the medication and was given pain killer through intra venous means. All the test were conducted including x Ray. The doctors suspected some tumour sort of thing below his large intestine. They asked his father whether any operation or surgery has been done on Ajit in the past. His father informed them about a major surgery done 3 years back and Ajit's Test paper and medical history was handed over to the doctors. The report was self-explanatory and it was revealed in the report that large intestine and area near scrotum was damaged and reproduction in male-organs may be affected and all depends how the parent reacts to the medication.

This opened Pandora's box in medical science. Some specialist were consulted and the area near scrotum and lower abdomen was opened and various tests were conducted. It was finally concluded by a panel of six surgeons that there is a severe damage in ejaculatory duct near seminal vesicle and the duct is partially blocked and twisted. It was also detected that his prostates glands are enlarged which are causing severe pain. He was operated for prostate glands which was a success but nothing could be done for his ejaculatory duct.

His father asked the doctors as what could be problems in future. The doctors very clearly told him that he will have no pain but whether he will become a biological father, is uncertain at this stage. May be some advance science is developed and even this problems could also be cured.

He was taken to ICU for post-operative care and then shifted to a normal room after two days.

He was to be discharged after 10 days. The doctor before discharging him, explained his total case history and asked him, Ajit do you have a girl friend? Yes doctor I have a girlfriend and we are supposed to marry after few months now otherwise it was next month.

Did you have sexual activities with your girlfriend any time since last three/four months. No doctor but yes, we did it once in our final year in IIT Bombay app two and half year back but why are you asking all this? Because there is damage to your ejaculatory duct which transports semen to vagina of a female and it appears that this may not happen and you may not produce kids in a normal sexual intercourse. But doctor, I remember it very clearly that when we had that last sexual activity everything was normal. I had, the desire, erection and discharge of semen.

The doctor explained to him that in most case there are no obvious signs of infertility. Inter-course and ejaculation will usually happen without difficulty but problem exists as Follicle stimulatory hormones F.S.H. lose control on bladder and sperms may not be transported properly to the vagina. Does it mean doctor, I may not become a father? I am not 100 percent sure but yes, there is a serious problem with your reproductory system.

Does my father know it? Yes he has been kept in loop from the first day. Where is my father now? Asked Ajit. He is outside only. We have asked him not to be present when we give you the case history and instruction on post-surgery care.

He was discharged from the hospital next day and given some sedatives to ease his sleep in this hour of anxiety.

Chapter 25

Ajit Under Post Operative Care

Ajit didn't have proper sleep and got up at 8 am and found his father in front of his eyes.

How are you feeling Ajju? Asked his father.

Ajit - Paa, does sudha know about my this problem. Yes son, she is a matured girl. She knows everything replied Vikram. What was her reaction? Asked Ajit. She only said. It is a sickness which can happen to anybody anytime. She was appearing graceful in saying this. Ajit's father replied. His father's answer and Sudha's statement proved to be a drop of water in OASIS to him. Ajit felt that this diagnosis affected not only me but my family and friends. I felt scared uncertain or angry about the unwanted changes, this sickness will bring to my life and theirs. I was feeling numb. I felt like shutting down myself mentally from the people around me.

Even since I have come to know about this, I am feeling shock disbelief fear, anxiety, guilt, sadness grief, depression anger and more. I do not know how would I handle this.

Am I becoming silent? It is natural to feel desperate upset that you don't believe the news. I am undergoing through a range of very strong emotions and these emotions are making me numb. These thoughts are becoming too harmful to cope with at all times.

I am unable to stop crying and worrying. I am even finding it difficult to look around and see life going on as normal for most people. I feel very strange to watch people going about their lives as usual. I also feel as if I am stuck under a huge black cloud. The feelings of sadness and depression are growing stronger with time.

What would he tell Sudha? How would he face her and react. He remembered his discussion with Sudha few days back when he said to her Sudha, we are financially ok for marriage but we have to save for our old age. He gave an interesting suggestion to her. He said every time, we make love. We will deposit One thousand rupees in our safe and whenever I say, I have one thousand rupees, you understand, what do I want. Sudha very coolly said if I agree to your this proposal, we will be multimillionaire by the time we retire. Now I give you a counter proposal, the day you don't have one thousand rupees, I will give you one thousand rupees. Do you agree to this proposal? Not at all said Ajit. This old memory further put him in more depression. He however always placed a very bold face in front of his parents and Shruti.

Chapter 26

Shruti came as usual to meet him. she was gracious about the fact that my infertility enigmas is a struggle stemmed from my physical condition and she knew me well enough by this time in our years of togetherness at home or otherwise. Ajit only asked Shruti, how could fate be so cruel to me? His world has come to standstill and has turned toppy turvy.

Trust yourself and have faith in God. You will be all right Ajit. Take this problems as a disease like any other diseases. Lord knows how tough the life can be. Ajit said to himself looking into Shruti's eyes. Nothing in this world is more powerful than love. Not money, greed, hate or passion. I love Sudha so much Shruti that I'll be long gone in the grave with her by my side and that love will still be burning bright.

Ajit, talk to Sudha, take her in confidence without being selfish Shruti told him. She is an intelligent girl and she is capable of using her mind over heart. Go with her and tell her that this is not a serious problem. I will share each and every thing with her and make her reason out for all her decisions. Shruti was made up of what material only she knows. She is absolutely selfless. She left with only one advice to Ajit. You do not share your grief with uncle, Aunty and Sudha. They are already disturbed beyond repairs. Yes, Shruti please keep on coming. I feel some strength after talking to you.

Chapter 27

Ajit Meets Sudha

Numb as I was and I also felt disoriented after that worst nightmare of my life. I knew the voice without thinking I got up and found Sudha standing right in front of me with sparking eyes, smiling face and most beautiful dress which I liked the most. Trust me the fragrance of Sudha and radiance of her face ignited my senses.

Sudha - How are your feeling Ajju now?

Ajit - Much better the wounds are healing and I have started walking inside the house. I will be visiting the doctor for removal of all stitches day after tomorrow.

Sudha - you look nice now. What about your diet and food etc.

Ajit - Mostly normal for few weeks I have to avoid red meat etc. how are you, uncle and Aunty?

Sudha - I am good, they too are good. My job is also good. Mummy Papa were asking about your health. They might call you tonight.

Ajit - Ok. Sudha, are you aware of everything of my this medical journey?

Sudha - Yeah, uncle has given me all the details including all that you want to tell me now.

Ajit - Sudha - I have to be honest with you specially about my inability to produce kids and probability of future complications of my prostate glands. Under the circumstances I think we should change our plans of alliance. I would also suggest that you talk to uncle and aunty and seek their advice. No parent would like to marry their daughter to an infertile man. Let us keep our emotions aside and think logic. Change the man.

I am used to change of residences due to my father getting frequent transfers from one city to another. But I am not used to change of men. You better understand it Ajit, Sudha told Ajit in anger.

Ajit told that if I explain to you that under what circumstance I am requesting you to refuse for this alliance, that's marriage, you would realize that Sudha, I am not a cheat but a victim of circumstances.

Sudha replied	-	I don't care what are your arguments in your justification for refusal, but at least tell or confirm that you are a man at least, that's good enough for me to go-ahead. Sudha was very aggressive and angry.
Ajit	-	Yes, probably I am not a man now.
Sudha	-	Relations never die a natural death. They are murdered by people like you who are disrespectful and disloyal to them. You get well soon we will discuss all this in details later.

Ajits parents entered and the conversation seized. Ajits father told Sudha that he is presently disturbed so do not take things to your head Sudha. There is time to sort out things. How are your parents? They are good. They will speak to you and Ajju to night. Sudha had lunch with than and Ajit had some clear soup.

Sudha left them with a bad taste but she also knew that Ajit is devasted and has no option left but to pick up the pieces and move on with his life but she definitely understood that she has to talk to her parents and use her or their minds rather than hearts.

Ajay Singh called up in the evening and talked to both Ajit and his father. Ajit told them about his health and said uncle I respect Sudha for her concern. I know that it is as difficult for her to forget about our relationship and of the period we spent together. I also know that she can deal with stress, carry heavy burden of emotions. She is very strong woman. She smiles when she feels like streaming, she cries when she is happy. Her love to me was unconditional. She only has one problem she forgets what she is worth. Why I am telling you all this because I need your help in explaining to her that it is going to be her life without Ajit because if I try to make her understand, she goes blank and goes inside the cell and counter argues with me with all possible medical solutions. I have had discussion with my own parents and even they have said that they would have not agreed for a marriage in case I would have been their daughter and Sudha as Ajit. All parents are so concerned about their daughters.

I do not know Ajit what all is going in her mind and what all she is passing in through. She is an army officer's daughter. Let me see what best is possible and how do I discuss these sensitive issues with her as father. Let me speak to your father. Ajit handed over the phone to Vikram. After exchanging normal pleasantries, both the fathers agreed to what Ajit has said. Ajay told Vikram that he will once again see them after talking to Sudha.

Chapter 28

Sudha to Ajay Singh

Before calling her father she composed herself, gathered courage and pretended to be normal. Papa how are you and mummy? Asked Sudha, we are ok beta how are you? Replied Ajay.

Sudha   - how was your discussion with Ajit's parents?

Ajay   - they were very cordial and discussed Ajit and you Sudha. I even talked to Ajit. He was sounding better, reasonable and in a state of cataclysm. There was clarity in his thoughts and he wanted to end this relationship. I could feel the agony, pain, anger in his mind for his this sorry state of affairs: But he showed his class of being human. Beta, he loves you too much and he is basically killing himself by trying to detach from you.

His father told me that Ajit has said that I have loved Sudha so much that I cannot see her in pain throughout her life. Our society will not raise fingers on me, they will all doubt Sudha for infertility. Agreed, she will have pain now but by leaving me she will not have it recurringly.

A j a y - continued   Beta, as far as we are concerned, we will go exactly the way you show us. As parents, we would, like to see you settled in life with kids and family. If you still decide to go-ahead with Ajit, we are with you as nothing is more dear to us except our own daughter.

Sudha said -   Ok. Papa, I would like to meet Ajit once, before I hand over the reins of my life to you both.

Bye mummy papa.

Bye Beta.

Chapter 29

Sudha With Ajit At His House

The next day she met Ajit. Ajit was recovering fast.

Sudha   -   Ajit you discussed all your apprehensions with Papa. Now you tell me, what is going on in your mind?

Ajit   -   Sudha, you know the situation better than me.

Sudha saw the parents coming towards them, Sudha requested them to leave both of them for a while which they gracefully did.

Sudha   -   Do you want to end this relationship Ajit just because you cannot father a child with me? How do you know that I would have had a child with you? I am not sure whether I am medically suitable to have a biological child.

The second thing medical science has so much of advancements that your this problem could be cured.

The third thing we can definitely have a child through IVF etc.

The fourth thing – In case a similar incident would have happened after our marriage, what would you have done? Would you have left me like that?

Ajit was speechless, he could give no answer to any of the question Sudha asked. He only said Sudha there are two reasons. One I cannot see you in pain even for a moment in respective of any reason. Be it social stigma or on emotional outburst. Two, a woman is created by God and she has some unavoidable biological needs and I do not want you to suffer on account of either or both.

I will have some pain now, you will have some pain but time will heal all these emotional wounds and I do not want to die a silent death in seeing you in a helpless stage. Ajit was firm and defiant.

Sudha - I am a strong independent woman. I have intelligence, inner strength and courage and will not settle for being a second choice like you marry me out of sympathy or so. I have loved you with all my heart and deserve true love and loyalty. She was equally firm and defiant. If that is intimidating to you, then you don't deserve my time, energy and me. I am leaving now and would wait for you. I am prepared to accept you in any condition including it even if you are terminally sick.

Yes, Sudha I have heard you but unfortunately I don't deserve you.

It was pathetic and pitiable to see both of them.

Chapter 30

Sudha Concluded

Sudha waited for two weeks for Ajit's response and finally decided to move on and leave Ajit on God's mercy. She said to herself that Ajit loved her beyond imagination and probably today also he is trying to part ways keeping my happiness in mind. I must respect his way of thoughts. He was a genuine lover. Break up definitely is a dreaded word and I don't know how people deal with it in the best way they can. Faced with the inevitable we both involved, should take a dignified route to ending the relationship and not indulge in public spat or ugly situations.

This question actually depresses me because I start thinking about some moments we spent together. She thought that someday we'll forget the hurt, the reason we cried and who caused us the pain. We will finally realize that the secret of being free is not the revenge but letting thing unfold in their own way and own time. After all what matters is not the first but the last chapter of our life which shows how well we ran the race of life so I will now smile, laugh, forgive, believe and love life all over again. This is not end of the world and you learn more about someone at the end of the relationship than at the beginning of it.

She called up her parents and informed them that I am single from now. I'll pursue some other challenges in life.

She also informed Ajit's parents.

Ajit only said that yes she has left deep affictions on my heart but she is right. He had a sleep of satisfaction for the first time after this incident and resumed work at Facebook the next day.

Chapter 31

Sudha Later After Break Up

She has to have courage to live. The challenges of daily life are often more difficult than those offered cataclysmic events. She thought to herself, whether to be honest, she has the courage and to do or say that when the truth threatens her physical intellectual or emotional security. She will recognize that her personal freedom depends on her ability to seek and find truth.

Whether she will remain ethical in this cynical world and resist temptations to be less ethical whether she will have courage to reject cynicism, whether she will have courage to assume responsibility for herself for the parents. She decided that she will a be courageous leader like one who is willing to change to grow and to make a difference and she will not be a bechari Mahila (poor lady). She transformed her life for Citibank, herself and her parents.

Ajit became a forgone and forgotten chapter and she moved on. This incident has left her disillusioned with the city and she got herself transferred to Delhi. She became quite strong and used to say that if any heart is in danger of terminal damage it is always yours so you do some hard thinking instead of hard chasing.

Chapter 32

After Six Months

One fine morning on Sunday Shruti noticed that Ajit was sitting in an apathetic, Gloomy and lonely mood. She felt that he may be affected due to clinical depression, she sat with him with some hot coffee for him.

Shruti: Good morning Ajit. She never called him Ajju like Sudha.

Ajit: Good morning Shruti. It is nice to see you and raise my spirits with this hot cup of coffee.

Shruti - Why were you so quiet and dull?

Ajit - Nothing in particular, was feeling a bit low. I remembered Sudha so a surge of anger ran through my nerves as I behaved so rudely with her.

Shruti: Ajit it is not only the love in this world, you have to think about all the time. There are more important things in life than that. You have your old parents to look after, you still have some professional projects to complete which are of national interest. You have friends to be happy with.

Ignite your passion for life. Reclaim your energy to work. Also Sudha, did not reject you.

You only loved her more by revealing your shortcomings. After passage of time she will only appreciate it. Please appreciate that you love God but he is bodily not present with you.

I am going in to help Aunty for cooking. You cheer up.

Ajit for a moment, was taken for a surprise that is it the same Shruti who normally is very quiet. Today she has given me the definition and meaning of life. She has drawn my attention towards her for the first time and ignited a small fire to feel that the ones who notice the storms in your eyes, the silence in your voice and heaviness in your head are the ones, you need to let in.

Ajit thought that his relationship with Shruti is a reaction to his life. Both of them are lonely and looking for something to fill this void. For him only time will make them come to terms with life. Deep down, he knows that this is just an episode in life and he will not be able to hold on to memory of Sudha for rest of his life. Sudha has a different future and Ajit will need it to let go. He thinks that let it not destroy his life with Shruti and lasting peace will come by seeking joy within. This will have him a deep understanding of his problem and resolution. A sprout of feelings towards Shruti was felt within by Ajit.

Chapter 33

After Two Months Relationship With Shruti

There is a certain relationship of mine which has been going on from last two months and Shruti is curious to know whether it is love or just a relationship based on sympathy. Honestly if it is second then I am confused whether it will sustain. Ajit thought it again and again. The confusion continues till Ajit knew that for Shruti there could most probably be a mixture of two. There are both sorts of feelings involved and he thinks sympathy is part of love. A relationship takes a lot of work and if you are together just for sympathy, then that's not a good relationship.

Sudha thinks that she is the one responsible for Ajit's condition and would not let him stay in mental guilt for which he is not responsible at all and Ajit thinks that this was just an accident or act of God for which he has no right to blame Shruti. Anyway they accept it as an act of destiny but decided to fight this enigma together.

Shruti was always a source of inspiration and mental strength for Ajit. Whenever she saw Ajit low on spirits, she always used to say that everyone goes through some hard times at some point. Life's isn't easy. Do you know Ajit that the people that are strongest are usually the most sensitive? Do you know the people who exhibit most kindness are first to get mistreated. So go on and also remember that sometimes, just because a person looks happy, you will have to look past their smile to see how much pain they may be in.

Ajit: Shruti you are a philosopher and a strong headed woman but I respect the humanity within. I now know why my parents have all the liking for you.

Shruti: This is a bit too much but I normally follow my heart which always helps me to think right.

Ajit: Why don't you marry and settle in life?

Shruti: I have my parents to look after and specially after my brother married a foreigner and cut himself off from all of us.

Ajit: Oh, It is basically a mirror image of events like I have my parents.

Shruti: I have my exam next month for IRS so I have to prepare for that.

Ajit: What is IRS? Indian Revenue service or Indian Railway Service.

Shruti: Indian Revenue Service which is mostly responsible for Income Tax, excise and customs.

Ajit: That sounds interesting so once you become an ITO, you will grant me relief in Income tax.

Shruti: You know me very well. I will never allow you to take advantage of my position in case it happens. On the other hand, I will have roving eyes for on all the people close to me for not defaulting on taxes.

Chapter 34

Anjali Discusses With Vikram

Ajit's mother was worried ever since his son's breakup and she was hesitant in asking Ajit whether he would marry. Before asking him, she wanted to know from Shruti whether she can marry Ajit and accept him as her husband in whatever circumstances, good or bad. Even before discussing with Shruti she discussed with her husband Vikram and wanted to know his views.

Anjali: Vikram, I was thinking of asking Shruti whether she would marry Ajit under these circumstances.

Vikram: Your idea is good, Anjali but do you think she will agree and Ajit will agree too and also tell me on what basis do you conclude that Shruti will be a good wife and a good daughter in law?

Anjali: I have noticed some qualities in her like she is optimistic and doesn't have any prior conception about us and Ajit. She is respectful to both of us. She advises us and seeks advice from us. She has her own mind and opinion but respects our opinion. She without any selfish motive takes me out for lunch and I feel a great degree of comfort level with her. She remembers our birthdays and anniversaries on the tip of her fingers and she makes us feel important on such occasions. She is responsible working woman and can take care of Ajit at all times. I have seen her standing like a rock of Gibraltar, when Ajit was shattered with broken dreams. Do you remember the time when earth was exploding, and sky was not existing for him.

Vikram: I know you are right Anjali. Go and talk to Shruti and her parents. Talk to Shruti first then to her parents. Please also understand that they do not have anybody except Shruti so their dependency level is quite high. Let me put it this way that in case this arrangement gets materialized both Ajit & Shruti will have two set of parents.

Anjali: Yes, let me first speak to Shruti.
Vikram: I hope the relationship between MIL
           & DIL is going to be much different
           than most of us have seen. MILs are
           generally perceived as monsters and
           assumed demons.

Chapter 35

Anjali V/S Shruti V/S Ajit

Anjali told Ajit to come home early today as I have called Shruti for serious discussion.

Serious discussion?

Yes, I am a mother and I have to see my son settled in life in any case. I have a very strong liking for Shruti so I will talk to her whether she can take care of my house including my son?

Maa, if you permit me, I would like to talk to her before you talk to her.

Ok but don't scare her with your wild assumption.

Yeah, Maa, I will be back by seven and I think that's the time, she comes home too.

Anjali fixed up the meeting at 8 p.m. as scheduled. She came five minute before 8.

Shruti: Aunty you all look very serious. What is the reason?

Ajit: I'll tell you. You finish your tea and let mumma go. There is something to be discussed between you and me.
Anjali left and started cooking for dinner.

Ajit: Would you marry me out of sympathy? Let me put it other way. I am physically challenged with some form of irreparable disability, you are aware of it. Would you still marry me?

Shruti: Basis of marriage should be love and no pity or sympathy. People say that marriage of this kind stand no chance of survival no matter how hard the couple try. Now my question to you Ajit is, yesterday you were a perfect guy. If I would have married you, yesterday or before this incident. do you think I would have left you or vice versa. So now or then my relationship is not based on beauty or money. It is based on two souls of eternal love and please understand that I have brought you to this status when you protected the modesty of a woman that's me. So why should I run away from such bad dreams?

Ajit: But Shruti I loved Sudha. She was my first love.

Shruti: You must have had a very short time to fall in love but will have life time to forget Sudha and she has taken more time to fall in love but less time to forget Ajit. Who says love doesn't happen for the second time? Sudha loved you with emotions. She did not love you with responsibility.

Ajit: I am not sure that I may father a child
            with you. How would you feel?

Shruti: The duty of a wife is not only to give
            you food or nice creased cloths as
            even a maid can do it but duty is to
            stand with you in all thick and thin.
            Yes, giving you biological children is
            a woman's dream and blessing but
            there are happy couple who do not
            have kids. We can always adopt a
            daughter or science has devised so
            many ways that we can even have
            our own kids.

Ajit: You are a winner. My mom will have
            some healthy pleasant moment with
            you today after so many months. My
            poor Maa. Thank you Shruti.

Chapter 36

Sudha At Citibank Delhi

Personal and professional ruin took a heavy toll on the life of Sudha. She knew that the problem or challenges are part of everyone's journey but they are catalysts for personal growth too. Sudha used this creative power of her mind to confront and shape them to reality. She knew her vision and involved her in all a activities of the office.

She kept the aim very high because she believed that everyone who has achieved greatness and fulfillment in life has started with a dream. She motivated herself towards her goal constantly even when at times her past was hunting and hurting her.

She went beyond her past and never again became a part of the problem. Sudha actually accepted and acknowledged the reality of situation. She healed and reconciled with future and renewed hope. Based on her hardwork she was promoted as senior manager at Delhi office of 'Citibank'. Now she had an opportunity to lead, supervise mentor and motivate others.

Her ability to do so effectively made a good difference to the success of the company.

She became a role model to the entire team. Her leadership was not about being domineering or tough on people. She set the goals for her as well for her team. She also shared all development plan with her team. She was effective even for difficult subordinates.

Based on her performance she was given an option to join Citibank LOS ANGELES U.S.A as general manager. In fact, she wanted to go away from India so she discussed with her parents and friends and accepted the offer. She informed Ajit's parents and left India in a fortnight. Both mummy papa supported her in all her endeavors. They once again asked Sudha if they try to find a right match for you Sudha which she politely declined by telling them, Mummy Papa, I'll let you know when the time comes and destiny, decides. They supported her this view also though they were not very happy with this decision. With a very heavy heart they bid a goodbye to their darling daughter. Vinita cried for months together.

Chapter 37

Ajit Weds Shruti

Anjali after talking to Shruti and understanding her resolution to wed Ajit asked her husband to call Shruti's parents at home in the evening.

Vikram - Mehta Saab, I understand that Shruti has informed you about her desire to marry Ajit after fully understanding the situation and medical history of Ajit. We would like to seek your blessing for them. There is absolutely no pressure on you or Shruti and you can always say no to this alliance if you do not agree. My wife has discussed with Shruti at length.

Mehta - Thakur saab, me and my wife are aware of everything. Shruti has discussed with us exactly on same times as she discussed with Mrs. Tomar. We are very much thankful to Ajit as he has risked his life for our daughter.

We are very fortunate that we have a daughter like Shruti who is a God's gift to us. She has a brilliant mind and a wonderful heart. She is a real human being to define humanity. She doesn't leave any scope of argument for us. She has a clarity of mind and thoughts. She has discussed all possible and not possible issues of Ajit which normally an Indian daughter cannot discuss specially with a father. Now with confidence, we can say that Shruti has taken a right decision of marrying Ajit and we now consider ourselves lucky to become your relatives. In fact God has been very kind to us by gifting us Shruti.

Vikram - We are fully convinced that they will make an ideal couple let us bless them. One more thing, I would like to share with you Mehta saab that after their marriage, you are part of this house and these kids will treat us as a set of two parents.

As far as the marriage celebrations are concerned, they will be done as per Hindu marriages of north India and you will be our guests. I have very strict instruction from my son that you will not make any arrangement. Your giving us Shruti is the biggest dowry of the world to us. Can we now have your permission to marry them in next 15 days?

Mehta -   Yes, Thakur Saab.

The marriage was fixed for 15th of this month as per the stars position and as per religious advice of Ajit's family Pandit. Gone are the days when horse carried the groom while Baraatis would dance throwing currency notes on him. Themed baraat is new attraction of Indian weddings and specially in a Rajput wedding. Ajit's marriage to Shruti was to follow all rituals starting from formal Roka ceremony to mehandi to Jaymala and taking vows around pious pyre. Both Ajit and Shruti were given traditional dresses, dance and music based on typical Rajputana culture. Though Ajit's parents followed all the rituals but they were on low key. The most interesting part was taking of vows in front of fire.

Ajit took all the vows and similarity Shruti also committed to all the vows. The main vows which, they took specially Ajit were.

1.   I will consider my wife to be better half. I will look after her just as I look after myself.

2.   I am accepting her as in-charge of my home. I shall plan things in consultation with her.

3.   I will never express dissatisfaction about any short comings in my wife.

4. I will always have faith in my wife. I will never look at another woman with a wrong intent.
5. I will be affectionate and treat my wife as a friend.
6. I will bring home all the income to my wife.
7. I will not criticize my wife infront of others.
8. I will have a tolerant attitude towards my wife.
9. If my wife is unwell or unable to fulfill some responsibilities I will not withdraw support or refuse to fulfill my responsibilities towards her.

Shruti also committed similar vows.

After these ceremonies they became husband and wife. All the functions were performed in Banquet hall of Marriot hotel near Ajits house and the Bidai also took place from Marriot hotel to Ajits house at Powai. Shruti's parents also accompanied their daughter. Vikram did not allow Mehta to spend anything on account of marriage expenses.

Shruti upon arrival was given a very warm, and traditional welcome by Anjali & her relations.

Both Ajit and Shruti were seen holding hands all the time till one of Ajits cousins told him that Bhai, leave her hand she is not going away from you. This caused a loud laughter across the drawing room.

Chapter 38

Ajit & Shruti On Honeymoon

After few day of marriage Ajit and Shruti planned to go to Nainital for their honeymoon. Shruti was nursing him to overcome his this anxiety symptoms while Ajit was struggling to fight his thought symptoms, Shruti was representing some powerful, truthful, expression of reality. She was always insisting and hesitantly explaining to Ajit that honeymoon is not all about repeated sexual encounters but it is to understand and make both the people compatible. Secondly there is nothing wrong with your performance except the discharge of semen due to damaged ejaculatory duct and enlarged prostate glands. She was quick to tell him that one of the ways, brains make problem, is the creative use of two most frequently used words and they are "WHAT IF"" second word is "WITH" that is determination to perform.

If you do not have problem like variation in heart activity, numbness, sweating, blushing, feeling weak, stomach upset, feeling hyper and feeling of unreality then everything is in your head so feel light and I am there na. Ajit asked, are you a doctor or what?

Shruti   -   No, I am just your nurse to nurse all your problems in life without even thinking twice about them. I am a woman first then a wife to you Ajit. I will keep you safe, well protected from all evils and dirty thoughts.

Ajit   -   Arre yaar, you are a magic pill in my life.

Ajit in his own words said that he felt that everything he did, every touch, every caress, every physical pleasure, she gave was all divine. If she touched him so he would die and then the thought crawled into his brains that if she didn't touch him then also he would die. The same was applicable to Shruti also. After she sat against him her hair ticking his face, he wanted Shruti to melt in him like butter on toast. He wanted to absorb her and walk around for rest of his life. Sudha confessed to him that everywhere you touched me Ajit, was a fire, my whole body is burning up and two of us becoming twin points of same bright while flame.

They then united in body and soul.

At this point his wife senses that Ajit is staring at her and Ajit opens one eye.

"What" she says

I say "What do you mean what?"

"What are you doing?"

"Nothing"

"What are you looking at me for?"

"I wasn't looking.... I was just thinking.... Are you really going to be right there every right?"

"Yes"

"Forever?"

"Mm.. hmmm."

"You are saying that of all the people in the world, the one to whom you will donate your naked self, night after night is me?"

"Yes, I have promised you that in one of the marriage vows."

Is it because I'm that appealing?" She now opens both eyes and asks Ajit to go back to sleep. The early morning sleep was just too too good. Next day Ajit took Shruti for a boat riding in Naini lake and enjoyed the beauty of green mountains surrounding the lake. After the boat ride, they had gone for shopping on the mall road. Suddenly the rains arrived with hail storm.

In a short time the entire mall road was covered with a white sheet of ice formed water and weather became too chilly but good to enjoy. They both had hot tea on one of the road side tea stalls. It was very cold in the rooms of the hotels and Ajit asked for a room heater.

It became very cozy with silk quilts and heater and it gave them both a feeling of being naughty. Ajit felt that Shruti was passionate lusty sensual firm wet, soft and powerful. It was enjoyed, appreciated, desired feared and confused. It is part of spirituality of relationship and it is a biological fact.

He subsequently spoke to Shruti in partly choked voice out of emotions and sexual act. Shruti, you have only taught me that this is all in the head and brain controls your performance in sexual encounters. I am now more or less recovered from that Phobia of not performing and not able to father a child. I will visit a doctor with you get myself reexamined. If there is slightest Lacunae, we will start the process of adopting a daughter.

Shruti -   Ajit, this is happiest and proudest moment for me to see my husband out of well of despair and no confidence. We will both take a call after talking to mummy papa and your in-laws also.

Ajit -   I knew that I have married a beauty with a more beautiful brains & hearts.

Chapter 39

Shruti At Work

Shruti like any working woman was still doing house work. She used to wake up at 5 am, hurried cooking breakfast, packing of lunch boxes for self and Ajit. rushing out to catch a train to reach her office at 9.00 AM. During the day, struggling with figures neglecting her own figure and return at 7.00 pm with a smile or her face to make everyone happy to see her. Her mom in law was doing all the house work including cooking lunch, getting the house cleaned, making tea for her husband at 5 pm sharp. She would do preparation of dinner but Shruti would never allow her except cooking some chicken or mutton. Shruti was a vegetarian in Toto.

She was making balance between her work in office and family life. Actually she had 24 hours day to perform. Even her office expected her to play multiple roll like care taken as professional and care taken at home care taken for ageing parents all four, was another priority for her. She was managing both the fronts by doing some planning, delegating, use of technology productivity efficiently. She used to set her goals and review them. There were always some slips pasted on her refrigerator to remind her as what is to be done today and tomorrow. She learnt the art of saying no specially to Ajit, if he made any unreasonable demand. By now she started showing an authority on Ajit. Poor Ajit, was singled out for not sharing house work with Shruti. No, it was not right on part of his parents to show partiality to Shruti inspite of Ajit helping each and everything. Soon, she became an apple of eye for both her and his parents. Still she was mostly caught in the trap of managing balance between work and home but over all she was most efficient, amazingly with such truthfulness and self-realization. This, she has achieved with maturity of age.

Ajit — Jokingly would ask Shruti whether she had any grudge against Sudha?

Shruti - I am not going to make you happy by answering this, the way you expect. I only respect her for her bold decision. Ok. I am slightly/ highly grateful to her as you are her gift to me. Are you happy with this answer?

Ajit   -   Yes, wifey. I would like to confess something with you today. Listen Shruti, I was in love with Sudha and you know about it. She was my first date but now I understand that not everyone you date until you meet the love of your life, is your soul mate. We all have an unconscious blue print of an ideal mate prescribed by God and your shear good deed of the past. I have passed process of hurting and being hurt and the process of finding a mate has been pretty scary. In the beginning, we are attracted to each other based on looks and mannerisms but in your case, it has become an exception as I feel that God has created you for me with a clear responsibility of taking care of a stupid guy like me. You have taught me that small changes in life yield big results. You have also taught me that emotions need to be expressed and contained. You are manufactured on my specifications.

Chapter 40

Two Years Passed

One fine morning Ajit and Shruti were having tea. Ajit in a simple white kurta, Pyjama and Shruti in a light pink Salwar Kameez. Ajit looked at her and said Shruti you are looking more beautiful, I am seeing a bliss on your face and radiance. May be after marriage you have become very attractive and tempting. Shuri only said, since mummy Papa are not at home so I would like not to understand your this Mumbo-Jumbo.

Ajit — No, I am not joking. I explain to you the reason of being beautiful after marriage. After marriage there comes a huge change in the lives of both husband and wife and especially for those who are truly madly or deeply in love. People, specially the women spend the fortune to look beautiful but there is an effective way that has enhanced your beauty and that is love making.

Love making can stimulate to feel good hormones, which in turn help in keeping the skin firm and glowing. It gives natural glow, sense of euphoria, shining and lustrous hair and reduces extra kilos. All these factors combined, have affected you and transformed you in a most beautiful woman.

Shruti -   Even you have attained few kilos on your body with a glow on your face.

Ajit   -   Yes, let us continue enhancing ourselves in all matters.

Shruti -   You only need excuses of sleeping with me. It is almost two years I have been noticing your these different intents.

In the evening we will all discuss about our planned adoption of a girl child. Let both the parents be part of our decision. Please ask uncle and aunty also to be present, Ajit told Shruti. They all sat together, discussed and after a good thought, we all decided that it was high time for us to adopt a baby girl, our daughter. Both Ajit and Shruti approached the agency CARA, central Adoption Resource Agency and as advised by them, they submitted all required documents along with the registration fee. They were informed by the agency within two weeks to contact them at their adoption center to see and finalize the girl child shortlisted by them. Ajit and Shruti decided that we are not going to select the child and reject any one. Their parents were heard murmuring whether the child is a muslim or Christian but the moment they gave Shruti, the girl child, all those feelings vanished and they simply sailed into the feelings of parenthood. First time when she looked at Shruti, she kept on looking at her. Tears rolled down and filed their eyes. That look changed our lives forever. She was only three months old, all wrapped from head to toe.

We accepted the child with open arms. All the basic formalities were completed and we brought our daughter home. Ajit was holding the little one in arms and Shruti was all in thoughts and said "when you are little I could hold you in my arms to comfort you but you will never be too grown up for me to put my arms around you. You are special to me and the most precious gift, I could have ever received, was you on the day you have come to our lives."

Ajit made a big poster on one of the walls of their bed room which read,

"If ever there is tomorrow,

When we are not together ....

There is something you must always remember.

You are braver than you believe,

stronger than you seem,

and smarter than you think,

But the most important thing is,

Even if we're apart ....

WELL ALWAYS BE WITH YOU"

They, means Ajit, Shruti, Vikram, Anjali and Mehtas named her CARA (BELOVED). Now for all of us she is CARA, CARA SINGH.

Chapter 41

Sudha At Citibank U. S.

Sudha over the time became so compassionate with work and life that she managed fear, hurt, loneliness rage and forgiveness. She forgave Ajit and achieved identity for himself. She became professional with spirituality. Sudha started reading Bhagavad Gita. Krishna outlined some qualities of a human to be merciful, obedient, truthful, equitable, saintly, magnanimous. Mild manner, clean, simple, charitable and peaceful. She surrendered her to God and became free of greed and possessiveness but remained steady and determined to her duties for both KARMA (office) and DHARMA (religion). By following above, she became a very successful professional. She used to tell to her and others that to maintain good character one must overcome KAMA (LUST) or selfish desire. Most of the people think that KAMA means just sexual craving but it simply refers to an overwhelming desire for anything such as lust for sex, lust for power, greed, dishonesty and corruption.

The influence of Bhagavat Gita on her was similar to what Arjun came out of depression and he got the boost in his declining morale, when he saw his friends and relatives in the battle field. He was demotivated before battle. Krishna gave him Gita Gyan (knowledge) which taught him to come out of relationship for a noble cause. Sudha, learnt the managerial effectiveness, approach from this and became a successful manager. She also took this Gyan as reference and gave up all her attachments to Ajit once for all time. She finally concluded that managers who are mentally weak, cannot attain the organizational vision and mission. Managers should use their intelligence to control the mind, they should not let the mind to be controlled by senses.

Sudha then became a professional with spirituality.

Chapter 42

Five Years Passed

Shruti was sitting in the balcony with her husband and her daughter CARA in Ajit's lap. He was continuously looking at her bundle of joy. Shruti is in the deep thoughts........ I know, I have no time to brush, no time to shower and no time to use the restroom. There is this tiny human being who takes up all my time and energy. Having said that the fact remains that motherhood is the best thing, that has happened to me. It is undoubtedly the most miraculous thing or earth.

Going back to how it all began......... the roller coaster ride that they describe motherhood as. So yes, I had an overwhelming first few months. Sometime I was clueless to what to do in a certain situation. The baby would Poop, Puke and Pee at the same time and I would almost pass out. But I learnt from every situation and with every passing months, I was turning into quite a PRO.

Every moment was reminding me of the unconditional love that our parents have for us, we take them for granted don't we? They tolerate our tantrums all the while. The only difference is they do it with their heart and Soul.

Time was flying too fast and she was growing up faster. Each day brought us surprises and precious moments. Then came one of the mile stones. THE MUMMA word uttered for the first time, albeit part of the usual babbling. Now I am sure, she is demanding my attention all the times.

Time doesn't wait for anything. She grew up and was admitted in KIDZEE, play group the lower KG, Senior KG and now in Ist standard of Marry Immaculate high school, Mumbai. She talks about her friends and teachers. The children are mystery and let us face it Ajit and what's going on in their little head is often baffling and hilarious. Ajit told Sudha let me find out from her how she sees the world at this tender age. I know that asking open-ended questions is a brilliant way to find out her interest and then bond her with family and friends.

Questions:

1. Cara who is your best friend?
   Milli is my best friend.
2. What do you want to become when you grow up?
   I want to become a doctor.
3. What is the nicest thing your friend has done to you?

She shares her tiffin box with me and I do mine.

4. Which game do you like the most?
   Cricket.
5. Are you scared of anything yes?
   The watchman uncle.
6. Who are you scared more mummy or Papa?
   Mummy
7. Why you don't like milk?
   If is not tasty.
8. Who is your favourite teacher?
   Sandra miss.

Shruti understood that she has her own mind. Both the parents just loved the conversation and enjoyed her childhood and their parenthood.

Chapter 43

A Happy Family

Ajits family was close knit family, his parents, Shruti's parents, his wife Shruti and the most important person CARA. They were very happy and content. They were the examples of successful family. On slightest problems of health of any of the parents or anyone, whole lot of family used to move the doctors and hospitals.

They were individual part of a successful family, which was identified and felt by the characteristics of each member their sitting together eating together and family interaction together, sharing duties and responsibilities together. They were economically self-sufficient. They enjoyed joy and stress together.

Some interesting things to share. Shruti was sitting in the car park in front of Ajit's office. They both planned to go for a movie. She waits and waits. Then something happens. She is bit irritated but suddenly she shifts the focus of her mind and thinks her husband to be hard working, responsible and excellent father and also a marvelous lover. You see him rushing around dictating one more brief letter, signing one more contract so he can drop it in the mail on the way to movie, returning the last call of the day so that he could devote his full attention to your evening together.

Your blood pressure decreases to the acceptable levels. Twenty minutes after the appointed time, she sees him coming through the double glass door of the tasteful office complex with fairly a good attempt to maintain a cheerful expression on his face. He jumps in the car and gave Shruti a peck on the cheek and says "I am really sorry I'm late. I had to finish up this contract so I could mail this on way to theatre.

He expects that Shruti will have confrontation, but Shruti just held his hand and said Ajit, you are sincere. Sometimes I forget to tell you how much I admire you, how successful you are at your career and how hard you work to provide me and the family. He melts, she melts and Shruti you do no less. I was expecting some fireworks but you simply and coolly gave me flowers. Thank you Shruti and I wonder which clay you have been made off by God? To make their family happy they all followed the advice of some genius of the past who said.....

"Success is living life on your own terms,
Living with people you want to live,
Working with people you want to work,
Doing the work you want to do,
Earning enough money to cover your expense,

Serving so many people as you can,
EVERY THING ELSE IS A COMPROMISE".

Shruti was the RIB of the family,
CARA was the reason for the nest.
This continued for another six year before .....

Chapter 44

Tragedy Doesn't Come Alone

After eleven years of blissful togetherness, one day Shruti came back from her office at 3pm with a twinge. She had an unbearable pain in both her arms. She hardly reached the bedroom and just informed Anjali about the sudden uneasiness, difficulty in breathing and pain in arms. By the time the medical help in form of a neighbouring doctor reached, she fell unconscious.

She was not responding to people and surrounding activities. The doctor arrived and after examination termed this as coma or comatose. He advised Ajit to treat it as medical emergency. He also explained the possible reasons. He said, Ajit, this might be due to hydration, low blood sugar. It can also happen due to serious heart and nervous systems problems. Please also check whether her fainting could be due to her taking too much strain or could be due to cough or breath disorder called hyperventilating.

He administered some intravenous medication to compensate for low blood sugar and conducted some breathing exercise called CPR. He further advised Ajit not to leave her alone as she might fall and injure her. Shruti recovered in senses in one hour. She didn't remember the sequence of events but felt too weak the doctor advised to admit her in hospital for further tests and treatment. Shruti was admitted to nearby Hiranandani Hospital very close to their house.

The doctors look her blood samples for chemical analysis. They also wanted to know from Ajit whether she had depression sometimes due to possible sadness, emptiness of any type. Ajit told them – No, not as yet.

The blood report was seen by a panel of doctors at Hiranandani, Blood sugar level were perfect. There was no problem for high B.P. all the cholesterol parameters were just normal. Timing for clot formation was also in acceptable limits. The only observation of blood sample, was not the uniform density. They were some clots observed. The doctor sent these blood samples report and fresh blood samples to Tata Memorial Hospital Mumbai for biopsy. This report came after two days and they found the presence of some cancer cell inflicting the blood with some suspected uneven molecular structure of the blood.

The authorities of Hiranandani advised Ajit to take her to Tata Momorial Hospital without any loss of time.

Fighting all his internal turmoil, composing himself, Ajit admitted her to Tata Hospital. There were too many questions Shruti asked as to why Tata Hospital? Were not satisfactorily answered by him. He only said some more advance tests are to be done which can only be done here.

Ajit - I could see some lines of worry and anxiety on your face, tell me I am a strong woman said Shruti to which Ajit turned his face, hid his expressions and said, but I am not a strong man. She was given a separate room in the hospital. This Hospital is considered to be specialist cancer treatment hospital, closely associated with Advance centre for Treatment, Research and Education in Cancer (ACTREC). It's famous for treatment of acute Lymphoblastic leukemia and has all the infrastructure like linear accelerator IMRT, Stereotactic Therapy, and HDU – BRACHY Therapy.

All the possible tests were conducted and all sorts of treatments were done such as Chemotherapy, Radio-therapy, surgery, biological therapy and harmone therapy and even the combination of above but she was not responding well to the treatment and it was expressly understood that Shruti was having advance cancer that cannot be cured as it is now secondary METASTATIC. Shruti was having a constant problem of Nausea. Fatigue, breathlessness and loss of hair.

Ajit didn't know how to break this news to Shruti and family. The reaction can often be mixed with other feelings such as fear, loss of control and even loneliness. By now Shruti has clearly understood her disease and was sinking towards depression but she was bolder than Ajit. She called her husband and asked him to close the door of the room.

Shruti – Ajit, we have spent close to 15 – 16 years together, 11 years as your wife and mother to CARA, Haven't you judged that Shruti can deal with stress, can carry heavy burden of life, I am not afraid of any things including death.

Ajit   -   Ok, but I can't leave you on destiny. I will take you to the best hospitals in world. I am selfish, I cannot leave you like that. How would I survive without you? What will happen to my daughter? Let us not talk on these lines and I am awaiting an advice from Dr. Krishan of U.S. to guide me for your further course of treatment tomorrow.

Shruti -   Do you know that we have loved each other for so many years and love has no age, no time and no death. You are my emotional sweet heart. Be practical in life and inform our parents. Be bold.

Next day, Dr. Krishan told Ajit that some people, improve and can keep disease under control for months and years without actually curing it. You can manage her pain with these Palliative medicines.

Is there any other way out doctor anywhere in world? Ajit asked the doctor.

I cannot assure you of her life but in case you want to take a chance, you can try few good cancer hospitals in LOS ANGELES U.S. for blood and marrow transplant. You can try Samuel OSCHIN Cancer Hospital, Cedars – Senai medical center and Keck medical Centre all in California State U.S.

Chapter 45

Preparation For U.s. Treatment

Ajit applied for six months leave and was granted leave with an open ended assurance for financial help by his employer Facebook. He informed his parents and Shruti's parents and explained that he has no option but to save Shruti at any cost. He will shake heaven and earth to do so. Nobody will weaken her, him or anybody. He only told CARA that her mumma is not feeling well and needs treatment in U.S. I will take her for some time and you stay with your grandparents and I will call you to come to U.S. in case it takes more time.

He knew that Sudha is in Los-Angeles since last 8 – 9 years. He never wanted to call her and seek her help as he has lost all moral rights to even bother her. He thought for a full day but he was mentally so weak and helpless that he called Sudha, to save Shruti even if he has to talk to his worst enemies whereas Sudha was his girlfriend, college and classmate and could have been his wife once. He also knew that Sudha was a reasonably a best human being and she would do her best efforts humanly possible.

Finally he called Sudha.

Ajit   -   Hi, Sudha, how are you? This is Ajit calling you from Mumbai.

Sudha   -   Hi, Ajit, what a pleasant surprise, how did you get my number?

Sudha   -   Tell me, how have you been for so long? How is everyone at home? How is Shruti? How is her job going on?

Ajit   -   Sudha, I need some favours. Shruti is suffering from blood cancer and that also in advance stage. I have tried the best possible treatment in Mumbai but she is not responding to the treatment. Now I have been advised to bring her to U.S. LOS ANGLES to any of the three cancer hospitals ie Samuel Oschin, Cedars-Senai or Keck Medical Centre. I have called you to please find out and help me select the best one. I have already applied for U.S. VISA.

Sudha   -   I am sorry to hear Ajit, give me a day's time to revert. All these hospitals are quite close to my place. I will try to make you comfortable for Shruti's treatment. If you need some financial help let me know. I would like her to recover well. Many critical patients have been cured here and the reputation of all three hospitals is very high.

I will take leave from my office and be with you. Trust me if you need anything I am just a phone call away. Please prepare to move and have courage.

Ajit got U.S. visa on priority based on medical grounds. Shruti was not much interested but she had to bow down to Ajit and they both reached L.A. in next 10 days and she was admitted on keck medical center the same day. Both Sudha and Shruti greeted each other with warmth. Sudha only said, it is unfortunate that we are meeting under these bad conditions but trust yourself and I trust Gita, we will meet as two healthy and close friends.

The treatment started after conducting all tests and medical reports of Tata Hospital. They examined her group and suitability of blood and marrow transplant. Luckily the group matched and the hospital had that in stock.

The blood and marrow were transplanted and she was kept under ICU for 48 hours. Ajit was given a moral boost by Sudha but the guy did not leave hospital till he was informed that Shruti is responding. Sudha had never seen Ajit so broken before. What else she could do. She was only standing with him like a wheel chair for a handicapped person.

Three weeks passed and Ajit was always told that she is fast recovering. He prayed in all nearby temples and did not eat property. He even called her daughter to be with her mom. What prompted him to do so, only he knows.

Chapter 46

That Inevitable

That inevitable was just around the corner, Death lay heavy. The doctors said "Shruti has only few hours to live. She wants to see her daughter. If you want your daughter to see her mother, she needs to come as quickly as possible. Ajit, I am sorry, let me say it again that we are dealing with few hours. Call me if need be. With these words, the doctor left the room. Ajit could only say "Thank you doctor". The night was rapidly approaching and he was a lonely man then he gathered courage and called Sudha to bring CARA.

How would I survive without her?

How would CARA deal with it?

He wept from the depth of his broken heart and broken hope. She has been such a splendid wife and mother. She is the one who has taken care of me, CARA and old parents. Cancer has reduced my lovely and healthy woman to mere skeleton on but her fighting spirit is still present.

CARA is just eleven years. She went in and closed the door to spend a little time alone with mumma. Shruti told her how special you have been to me my daughter Get your Papa in.

Ajit you have been a wonderful and an ideal father. Promise me that you will be a mother also to my darling daughter and start going to temple which you stopped since months. I have noticed that you have lost faith in God. Please do not do that and take my daughter also to the temples with you.

Mumma, don't worry. I will take care of papa, the way, you were doing and I will take him to temple. After all I have DNA of both of you. Poor thing, she didn't even know that she is an adopted child.

Few moments later mumma became a body. He took the small lady of his precious wife in arms and they both wept openly together and deep within tears rolled down Sudha's eyes. Sudha made all the arrangement for bringing Shruti in body no life back to MUMBAI.

Ajit came back to MUMBAI with his daughter CARA ....

She was his life line thereafter.